the Mae West Murder Case

GEORGE BAXT

the Mae West Murder Case

ST. MARTIN'S PRESS
NEW YORK

Production Editor: David Stanford Burr

Design: Basha Zapatka

Library of Congress Cataloging-in-Publication Data

Baxt, George.
    The Mae West murder case / George Baxt.
        p. cm.
    ISBN 0-312-09864-2
    1. West, Mae—Fiction. 2. Motion picture actors and actresses—California—Los Angeles—Fiction. 3. Serial murders—California—Los Angeles—Fiction. 4. Hollywood (Los Angeles, Calif.)—Fiction.
    I. Title.
PS3552.A8478M34   1993
813'.54—dc20   93-20791
                                           CIP

First Edition: December 1993

10 9 8 7 6 5 4 3 2 1

for
Margaret Longbrake

ONE

"IT WAS SO NICE HAVING YOU," said the slightly tipsy hostess.

"Honey, it was nice being had by you." The voice was unmistakably familiar. Seductive, mocking, sinuously sincere.

"You're sure you don't want me to call a taxi?" she asked eagerly. "It's terribly late."

"I don't live too far from here, honey. I could use the walk. G'night, dear."

"Nighty night!" The hostess shut the door and slowly slumped onto the foyer floor, a very silly look on her very ordinary face.

The full moon was playing peek-a-boo through the palm trees. Los Angeles is lousy with palm trees. The trees are hollow and inhabited by families of rats. Palm trees were imported to Hollywood and its environs some forty years earlier by a shrewd real estate developer. The lady slowly making her way home to her cottage on Highland Avenue in West Hollywood was also a shrewd operator. For her appearance at the party she'd collected one hundred dollars. She would have done it gratis just for the opportunity to try out the new material she'd been rehearsing for an upcoming cabaret appearance.

Around her neck was draped a feather boa, artfully arranged. Her hands were each on an undulating hip. Softly she sang to herself, "Frankie and Johnny were lovers, oh yeah."

1

It was two in the morning. Highland Avenue was deserted. She knew every other street in town would be deserted. Most of the time in broad daylight they were deserted. Los Angeles was an automobile town. Public transport was a joke. Los Angeles was a joke. Without the movie studios, Hollywood would be a ghost town. The studios were on an upswing. The Great Depression was still worrying in this year of 1936, but the president of the United States, Franklin Delano Roosevelt, was doing a great job in trying to restore a healthy economy. She listened to his "Fireside Chats" religiously on the radio, and that charming voice of his enchanted and reassured her.

Her handbag hung from her right wrist. It swayed back and forth like a pendulum. She reached the paved walk that led to her veranda. Damn. She could have sworn she'd left the veranda light on when she left for the party. She rummaged in her purse and found the front door key. She thought she heard a rustle of the tall hedges that lined the paved walk. She turned around and gasped.

It was as though he had materialized from her imagination. He wore a black cape with a cowl that covered his head and obscured his face. His hands were outstretched and holding the ends of the cape, giving him the appearance of a grotesquely obscene bat.

She wasn't afraid. She was amused. All her life she'd dealt with men. It never occurred to her that one day she'd come up against one who was dangerous. He said nothing. He just stood there. A light breeze caused the outstretched cape to flap slightly.

"What's your pleasure?" She was bravely cheeky.

He moved forward slowly. She wondered what would happen if she screamed. Her neighbors on the right were an elderly couple, and both were more than slightly deaf. Her neighbors on the left owned a bar and grill in downtown Hollywood, and she doubted if they were home yet. Patrol cars in the area were nonexistent.

"Now listen, honey, if this is a practical joke, I don't get the pernt." She was amazed at how calmly she spoke. In a flash it occurred to her this might be her rotten ex-husband in disguise, here to rob her. She'd spoken to him earlier that evening and told him she was doing a private party. "Cut it out, Louis. You ain't gettin' a nickel." The moon held his right hand briefly in the spotlight. She glimpsed the ring, that awful ring, the ring that was coming at her, a bat's head with two protruding fangs. He swooped at her, pushing her to the ground. The fangs punctured her throat. His left hand moved quickly and she sighed as the knife blade entered her flesh and penetrated her heart. She stared at the sky with a look of astonishment. This was not the way she had planned to die. She had expected to live into her eighties and expire in her sleep from the excitement of one last gratifying sexual encounter.

Even though life was leaving her, she shivered as she felt his mouth cover her wounded neck and lap at the blood seeping out, lapping like her greedy Pekingese when she put a saucer of chicken soup in front of it. Oh God, oh God, it feels so good. Dyin' ain't all that bad after all. What a way to go.

The following morning, Penelope Granger was walking her mutt Wilhelmina, its pedigree one of infinite variety. It was shortly after seven A.M., and Penelope and Wilhelmina were having their usual disagreements. Wilhelmina would pull Penelope to a lamppost and Penelope would rudely jerk her back. "Not that one, Wilhelmina. I know you mutts leave each other messages when you pee, but that big mastiff does his there and I keep telling you he's much too big for little you, and what's more, he's uncouth. He slobbers. How about this nice palm tree?" But Wilhelmina had a mind of her own. There was something interesting lying on the paved walk to her right, and she had every intention of investigating it. She lurched up the walk, pulling Penelope behind her. Caught by surprise, Penelope lost her grip on the mutt's leash and almost fell forward onto the paving.

"You rotten bitch!" Penelope yelled as she struggled to regain her balance.

Wilhelmina was oblivious to the string of nasty epithets

3

raining around her like a salvo of darts from a tribe of angry savages. She was sniffing a lovely perfume and contemplating grabbing in her mouth the feathered boa lying alongside the body even though it was stained with blood.

Penelope Granger was momentarily frozen to the paved walk. A hand flew to her mouth. The body lay in a grotesque sprawl, eyes wide and staring but not seeing. Penelope was staring at a buxom blonde who had what used to be known as an hourglass figure. Her dress was more appropriate to the era of the Gay Nineties. Her handbag was beaded and cheap. Her neck was wounded and the blood had coagulated. Penelope went closer for a better look at the face. She knew this person. She adored her. She was so wicked. So funny. Always kidding herself and kidding her audience. Oh, my. It can't be. *She's dead. She's been murdered.*

Penelope opened her generous mouth and screamed, *"Mae West is dead! Mae West's been murdered!* Help! Police! Somebody murdered *Mae West!"*

"Of course it's not Mae West," said detective Herb Villon to his younger associate, Jim Mallory. "Nobody murders Mae West except some critics."

"You could fool me," said Jim Mallory. "This one's a perfect look-alike."

The detectives had learned from a middle-aged couple who said they owned a bar and grill that the victim's name was Nedda Connolly. The couple were Ross and Audrey Ditmars. Audrey Ditmars told them, "She does Mae West impersonations for a living. She was pretty damned good too. Poor thing. She was booked to open in a couple of weeks at some crib in Santa Monica. It was tough getting the booking—there's so much competition in Mae West impersonators."

"It's easing up," said Herb Villon with an edge to his voice. "She's the third impersonator found murdered in the past four months." The preceding two were males, Larry Hopkins and Danny Turallo. While examining the late Mrs. Connolly, the coroner told the detectives that the modus operandi was the same as the previous murders: puncture wounds above the jugular vein, a fatal knife wound to the heart.

"It appears that somebody really doesn't like Mae West impersonators," said Villon to no one in particular.

"Maybe it's Mae West," suggested Jim Mallory.

Villon said, "Mae West kills people, but her weapon is her tongue. What has me worried, will these killings multiply?" He asked the Ditmars, "You didn't hear her scream?"

"We didn't hear anything. We didn't get home until after three this morning. We closed the bar at twelve as usual, sometimes earlier because it's downtown and you know that place is a morgue after the movie houses empty out. Then we played poker with the bartender and a couple of the waiters. She must have died before we came home."

"What about the people who live in the house on the other side?"

"Very old and very deaf and they go to bed very early," Ross Ditmars told Villon.

Villon wondered aloud, "How come their curiosity hasn't brought them out here?"

"Oh, they're curious all right," said Audrey. "They're peeking out at us behind their blinds. They're very timid. You can try talking to them but you won't get anything. Not anything useful, I don't think."

Jim Mallory had busied himself examining the hedges. "He hid behind these hedges. Look. Some twigs are broken."

"Any footprints?" asked Villon.

"Smudged."

"Poor, poor Nedda," said Audrey Ditmars. "What will become of her canary and her mutt?"

"Lady, that's the least of my worries. What about men? Did you notice any men in particular visiting her?"

Audrey Ditmars drew herself up to her full five feet and said smartly, "We are not snoopers. I don't park myself at the window to spy on my neighbors."

Ross Ditmars interjected, "There was that rat Louis."

"Who's Louis?" persisted Villon.

5

"Her ex," said Audrey. "Small change. Poolroom hustler. Always after her for money. If you check our local precinct you'll find she had him arrested a couple of times for trying to beat up on her."

"Sounds charming," commented Villon.

Audrey smiled a very small smile. "Oh, he was a winner, a real winner. Ross here"—indicating her husband—"worked him over once."

"That was a real pleasure," said a beaming Ross.

Villon said to Jim Mallory, "Give her place the usual working over. Get some boys here quick. I doubt if we'll find anything of any importance, but tell them to go through the motions anyway."

Some reporters and photographers had arrived. While Villon told the reporters what little he knew, the photographers were directed to Penelope Granger and her faithful friend Wilhelmina, who had been sitting quietly on the porch steps waiting for Villon to dismiss them. Penelope was delighted to pose while telling the reporters how she and Wilhelmina had discovered the body.

One reporter asked Villon, "Hey, Herb, you think you got a Jack the Ripper on the loose?"

"I doubt if it's Jack the Ripper. But it's somebody equally good. Real good."

Another reporter who was slightly intelligent said, "Them puncture marks on the neck. They coulda been made by, you know, fangs maybe? Like maybe it's a vampire like Dracula?"

"Looks like it, doesn't it," said Villon. "Well, boys, we all know there are lots of vampires in this town. And if they can't sink their teeth into your neck, they'll sink into something equally vulnerable."

Jim Mallory asked, "I wonder what Mae West thinks of these murders. Do you suppose they're making her nervous?"

Mae West's apartment at the top of an all-white building in central West Hollywood covered the entire floor. It was beautifully furnished and decorated in white. She adored white. Her lovely skin was pure white. In dress, her preferences leaned to navy blue and other dark shades of blue, or black. Although she gave the illusion of height, she was actually surprisingly short of stature, barely an inch or two over five feet. To add to her illusion of height, she wore shoes cleverly constructed to add four or five inches to her five feet one or two. Only her few intimates recognized that because of this she had to amble about cautiously, moving one foot in front of the other very slowly and carefully so she wouldn't fall flat on her face. It was this slow, careful look she so cleverly developed that caused her hips to sway, her body to move so lithely and supplely, and lo and behold, there emerged the world's most notorious sex symbol.

On this sunny morning, with the sun pouring into the all-white living room, the sex symbol reclined on the white couch chatting with a visitor. The visitor was Agnes Darwin, and where the room and its hostess was all bright and cheery, Agnes was all dark and gloomy. In contrast to Mae West, Agnes was angular and bony. A black turban obscured even blacker hair. Her eyes were almost hidden by lids heavy with black kohl, the eyes themselves a piercing green brown. She wore a long purple dress that reached to her ankles, hanging so loosely she looked shapeless. From her ears there dangled two unique earrings that she herself had designed, witches on broomsticks that looked decidedly menacing. Her long, dangerous-looking fingernails were polished in deep purple. Though her hostess disapproved, she smoked a Turkish cigarette in a long purple holder. One of Mae's two black maids entered, rolling a tea cart that held carafes of tea, coffee, and cocoa. There were plates of assorted biscuits and clever little bite-size sandwiches of cucumber and butter. Mae explained to her guest, who commented on the sandwiches, "They're an acquired taste, honey. I acquired them from an English lover back in New York in twenty-five or twenty-six. He was on the lam from Scotland Yard I later learned after I dumped him. Last I heard of him he was doin' time on Devil's Island, the old devil. Help yourself, Agnes.

Desdemona"—to the maid—"you do the honors. What's your perzon, Agnes, tea, coffee, or cocoa?"

"No gin?" The voice was baritone.

"Now, you know I don't keep no licker in my jernt. Maybe a little brandy for medicinal purposes, some beer for some of the boys. Drink killed my father, God rest his soul, and smokin' that Turkish manoower is gonna kill you. Put that cigarette out, or I'll choke to death. Tea for me, Desdemona. What's Goneril up to?"

"She's preparing lunch."

Agnes indicated the tea cart. "So what's this?"

"Breakfast," said Mae. "Actually, I'm expectin' a couple of detectives."

Agnes's eyes narrowed. "You're in trouble?"

"Me?" She smiled with her eyes twinkling. "Why, Agnes, one way or another, I'm always in trouble. But it's the kind of trouble I enjoy. Y'know, back in twenty-six I did eight days in the pokey on Welfare Island . . . that's in the East River in New York in case your geography's weak. I was sent up because of the play I wrote and starred in, *Sex*." Agnes looked startled. "*Sex* was the name of the play. A bunch of bluenoses blew the whistle on me. So they arrested me and sent me up. I had a great time. Met some real great gals. Prostitutes, shoplifters, and oh yeah, one really funny gal who perzoned her husband and her three kids. She was plannin' to write her memwahs. I don't know if she ever did. Anyway, I'm digressin'."

She sipped some tea, told Desdemona it was excellent, and sent her back to the kitchen to help Goneril prepare the lunch. "These here detectives are after the killer."

"What killer?"

"The one knockin' off my impersonators. They think it's all a warm-up to knockin' *me* off. I've been gettin' weird phone calls. No conversation. Just heavy breathin'." She was on her feet and pacing, irritated at the thought of impending death. "Nobody's killin' me. I got too many plans. I want to do grand opera, y'know, like I did in *Goin' to Town*, singin' Delilah."

"You called that singin'?" asked Agnes, who would never be known for subtlety.

"Listen, you, you're supposed to be a witch, not a bitch. Yeah, that was singin' as far as I was concerned. Now, where was I? Oh, yeah. My plans. Then I want to play Catherine the Great on Broadway. I got a whole new angle on her, not like Marlene did in that rotten picture of hers, *The Scarlet Empress*. Anyway, I'm sexier than Marlene."

"That's open to discussion." Agnes heard the door chimes playing "Frankie and Johnny," the song Mae had performed with such brio in her second film, *She Done Him Wrong*.

"That must be the detectives." Mae hip-swayed her way to a white throne chair, settled into it, arranging her black hostess gown artfully. She sat upright with an insinuating smile, looking every inch a queen.

Desdemona entered and spat the word "Fuzz." Villon and Jim Mallory followed her into the room.

Mae recognized Villon and her face lit up. "Why, Desdemona, this ain't no ordinary fuzz. These are old buddies whose names I can't remember." Villon refreshed her memory. "That's it, Villon like in Frances Villon who wrote poems, and Mallory like in Boots Mallory what's married to Jimmy Cagney's brother. Arrange yourselves near the tea trolley, boys, and have some refreshments. This here over here is my friend Agnes Darwin. You may have heard of her. She's a genyoowine authentic witch. You might have noticed her broomstick parked in the hallway." Agnes was annoyed and showed it. "I'm gettin' myself interested in witchcraft because I've got some thoughts on playin' one in the near future." Jim Mallory was absorbed in studying the bizarre Agnes Darwin. Herb Villon was absorbed in the luscious forty-four-year-old Mae West. Although he didn't actually know her exact age, he knew she was surely making inroads into middle age. West interpreted the look on Villon's face correctly, wiggled insinuatingly, and said, "A dollar for your thoughts."

Villon felt himself blushing. He smiled, asked Mallory to pour him some coffee, and then told Mae about Nedda Connolly's murder. He heard Agnes's half whisper "Puncture marks."

"Above the jugular. The kind of marks I suppose would be left by a vampire."

"Puncture marks," Mae said thoughtfully. "I'm not unfamiliar with puncture marks. But I ain't familiar with vampires. Not the kind Bela Lugosi plays. They don't exist," she said with a disdainful wave of a hand.

"But they do exist," Agnes said darkly, and Jim Mallory suppressed a chill. "There are blood worshippers scattered throughout the world. Believe me, Mae, they do exist and they do drink blood. They don't drain bodies of every drop."

"No? They don't want to make pigs of themselves?"

"There was a cult of blood worshippers exposed in Mexico only a few years ago, and I've heard of a cult that's flourishing right here in Los Angeles." She said to the detectives, "They might have something to do with your murders."

Mae got to her feet and paced. "Well, it sounds to me like all they do is drink the blood of these poor kids impersonating me. That Hopkins boy was damn good. I saw him at the Club Honky Tonk and it was like watchin' myself in a mirror. What the hell's goin' on, Herb?"

"Mae, have you any enemies?"

"Only the censors. The Legion of Decency's been after me ever since *She Done Him Wrong*. And *I'm No Angel*. Now, you seen me, ain't you, boys? Do I do anything obscene or pornographic?"

"No way!" thundered Jim Mallory, a dyed-in-the-wool Mae West fan. Villon shot him a look but Mallory ignored it.

"They keep denouncin' me from the pulpit all across the country when all I'm sellin' is good clean raunchy fun. Hell, my pitchers along with Bing Crosby's and Cecil B. De Mille's rescued Paramount Pictures from the brink of bankruptcy. For cryin' out loud, De Mille's pictures have more sex in them then mine. Y'know, I've written Roosevelt that I could rescue us from this depression if he'd bring me into his cabinet as secretary of sex." She took a moment to simmer down. She saun-

10

tered to where the detectives were sitting. "Say, boys, do you suppose this here killer vampire, whatever he is, is sendin' me a message? Hmm . . . . I wonder if Frank Wallace is in town."

Villon was interested. "Who's Frank Wallace?"

"Some son of a bitch I married when I was nineteen years old, and don't ask me what year *that* was."

"I know the year," Agnes said smartly.

"You do? Well, keep it under wraps or you've cast your last spell." Mae said to the detectives, "Frank's an oldtime song-and-dance man. I hear from him every now and then, usually when he's short of the green stuff and tries to shake me down. One of these days I'll get a divorce. Say, do you suppose he's doin' them heavy breathin' phone calls? Ahh! It can't be Frank. He never once tried to bite my neck." They heard the door chimes. "That'll be my personal manager, Jim Timony, and my personal bodyguard, Seymour Steel Cheeks. His father was a genyoowine Cherokee Indian. His mother was a genyoowine Greek belly dancer. They met in Athens thirty years ago when Seymour's father was touring Europe with Buffalo Bill's Wild West show." James Timony and Seymour Steel Cheeks entered. "Come on in, boys, and meet some old friends." After the introductions, Mae explained there was another murder. "That's four murders so far."

"Three," corrected Villon.

"Four," insisted Mae. "A nice kid found dead in Griffith Park was first. He did an impersonation of me and a pretty good one too, though a bit overpadded, I thought. He wasn't in costume when they found his body, which is why you may not remember. He called himself Neon Light."

Mallory interjected, "It rings a bell." He reminded Villon, "We were on the call girl murders at the time."

Villon said, "I remember now. There was nothing special about the murder. No puncture marks on the neck, just a bashed-in skull."

"Puncture marks or no puncture marks," said Mae, "he impersonated me and I think he deserves a place with the other three."

"Jim," said Villon, "let's dig into his file and see if this Neon Light ties in."

Mae was at Seymour Steel Cheeks's side and gently squeezing an arm muscle. "Oh, my, I think I'm feelin' a new one."

Steel Cheeks said with pride, "I only developed it this week." He added shyly, "I call it Mae West."

"Well, how about that!" She explained humorously, "Seymour names all his muscles for movie stars. He's a dedicated body builder and a faithful movie fan. I'm really flattered." She felt the muscle again. "Well, folks, now you've really seen Mae West squeeze Mae West. Whaddya suppose the Legion of Decency would say to *that*?"

TWO

A FEW MINUTES LATER, MAE SAT on the couch next to Agnes Darwin, buffing her nails. She addressed Timony, her manager, who was portly, Irish, Brooklyn born, and chronically frustrated by Mae's rebuffs of his unwanted amorous entreaties. "Whaddya think, Jim? You think these murders are leadin' up to an attack on me?"

"Is that what Mr. Villon and Mr. Mallory think?" He was aching to light a cigar but knew if he did, Mae would exile him from the apartment.

"They ain't said it for sure, but I know they're entertainin' the idea. Right, boys?" Neither corroborated her statement. "Sure you think it and Agnes thinks it and Jim thinks it and I think it. And that's a majority. Who's behind them phone calls might be the killer. And it has to be someone I know because I ain't listed. Right, Herb?" Herb agreed.

Seymour Steel Cheeks spoke up. "Anybody lays a hand on you, I'll break every bone in his body."

Mae smiled. "Ain't he adorable. From the first time I laid eyes on him in the ring, I knew I had to have him . . . um . . . work for me. He's one Indian for whom I happily circle my wagons." She caught a look of concern on Villon's face. "What's botherin' you, Herb?"

"You're too exposed."

"You think so? I'm wearin' one of my more conservative outfits."

"I mean you're too easy a target."

"You think Seymour ain't enough protection? I can hire some more. Jim, get me more bodyguards. Call a couple of gymnasiums and have them round up a lot of muscle for auditions this afternoon." She advised the detectives, "I got the day off today. I'm shootin' my new box-office bonanza, *Go West, Young Man*. Clever title, right? It's from this here hit play, *Personal Appearance*. They had to change the title."

"Why?" asked Agnes.

"Well, can you imagine the marquees across the world advertisin' Mae West in *Personal Appearance*? They'd think I was there in the flesh. That kind of a mistake could cause riots." The chimes rang. "I gotta get them chimes changed. I'm sick and tired of 'Frankie and Johnny.' Every time I go to a club the orchestras play it when I make my entrance and it's getting boring. I think I'll change it to 'Easy Rider.' " She chuckled. "I also sang that one in *She Done Him Wrong*. You know that French expression double intended?"

Agnes said smugly, "You mean *double entendre*?"

Mae's eyes signaled red. "Ain't that what I said?" She said to the others, "It means it has a double meanin', and boy, did that one have a double meanin'." She sang suggestively, "Ohhhhh . . . I wonder where my easy rider's gone . . . ohhhhh" and broke off as Desdemona entered. "Who is it, honey?"

"Father Riggs."

Mae said through a laugh, "It's a good thing I didn't sing the rest of it. The clergy's here. Send him in, honey. Say, Jim, you notice Desdemona and Goneril have taken to imitatin' my walk."

"They love you," said Jim. "You should be flattered by their devotion."

"Ahhh! I think they think I've got a touch of the tar brush in me. Well, maybe I do. I used to be what they called a 'coon

14

shouter' in vaudeville, y'know, singin' the kind of lowdown jazz that appealed to the nigras.'' She chuckled again. "I sure do love them. I sometimes think they know me better than I know myself. They certainly have the same bad taste in men that I have. Oh, hello there, Father. Come on in, sit down. Delilah!'' she shouted. "Bring me my checkbook, my bottle of ink, and my quill!'' To the others she said, "This here's Father Riggs. Wallace Riggs. He rules the roost at my local diocese. He gives great sermon.'' Father Riggs sat on a straightback chair, his face wreathed in a saintly smile. "Look at that handsome face, look at them shoulders. He should be in pitchers himself.''

"You always say that, Mae. And I keep telling you get me a screen test and if I make good, I'll gladly go into pictures.''

Agnes was enchanted by his dimples.

Mae crossed her legs. "You'd really give up the pulpit for the silver screen?''

"It pays better.''

"It sure does. Pitchers have made me rich. I bought this buildin' only a month ago from last year's earnin's. And Jim's a pretty good manager. He gives good investment. So tell me, Father, you got any theories on these here impersonator murders?''

"God rest their souls,'' he intoned as Delilah entered with a serving tray that held Mae's checkbook, a bottle of ink, and a quill pen.

"Never mind their souls, tell me what you think.'' She said to the others, "Father Wally's a real smart cookie. One of these days he'll be pope. My money's on you, Father.'' She had crossed to a white desk and was writing a check. "This ought to hold you for a while.''

"You're a wonderful, generous woman, Mae.''

"I'm the most wonderful, generous woman walkin' the streets.'' She tore out the check, waved it to dry the ink, and gestured to Father Riggs to take it. As he crossed the room to her, Mae urged, "Now come on, Father, tell me what you think.''

"I think the murderer is a godless fiend.''

"You mean like Adolph Zukor, my boss at Paramount."

Villon spoke up. "Do you believe in the existence of vampires?"

"While I have enjoyed reading mythology in my youth, I do not believe in the supernatural. There are no vampires, there are no ghosts, and there are no witches."

"I beg your pardon!" fumed Agnes. "*I* am a witch and I'm a damned—oops—good one."

"I don't know about that, Agnes," interjected Mae. "That last cauldron of soup you made had too much eye of newt."

"This is not a laughing matter, Mae. I am a witch, my mother was a witch, and her mother before her and so on ad infinitum. My family dates back to the Middle Ages when several aunts and uncles were burned at the stake. You see, Father, you too suffer from a misconception about witches. Witches do *good*. At least most of us do. Oh, every now and then I cast a little evil spell on someone who annoys me, such as my butcher when he sells me inferior meat, but that's really only to keep in practice."

"How's about castin' a spell on this murderer?" suggested Mae.

"I can't cast a spell without his picture and a lock of his hair and some of his nail parings." She was torching a cigarette. Suddenly her eyes widened. "Oh my, oh my no."

"What's the matter, honey? Them cucumbers repeatin' on you?"

"What? I—I'm sorry. I had a sudden spasm. I get them occasionally. They pass quickly." She finished lighting her cigarette, while subtly her eyes moved from individual to individual.

"The ball's back in your court, Father," said Mae. "Do you have a theory? The boys here"—indicating the detectives—"share my suspicion that I'm the killer's real target. These four murders are just a warmup, you know, like a show tryin' out out of town before opening on Broadway."

Father Riggs asked her, "Have you any idea why anyone would want to kill you?"

"Well, yeah, sort of, come to think of it." Mae was pacing the room again. "It's got to be some kind of a nut. Maybe a religious fanatic sort of. We're not kiddin' each other, Father, you're one of the few clerics who hasn't denounced my morals. Why, from time to time *I've* even denounced my morals"—she smiled insinuatingly—"especially when I'm in the path of temptation. And there's nothing so temptin' as temptation."

Father Riggs was deep in thought. "The only connection between the three unfortunates was that they earned their living impersonating you." He paused. "Did they know each other?"

Villon told him, "Larry Hopkins and Danny Tuvallo were acquainted. We don't know if either or both of them knew Nedda Connolly. But, Father, there was a fourth victim, we learned from Mae."

"A fourth?" Father Riggs wore a startled expression, as though he might have just heard Judas Iscariot was thoroughly misunderstood.

"Yeah. A nice kid who performed under the name Neon Light. I never knew his real name. After seein' me in my first couple of pitchers, he became a big fan of mine. Wrote me a very sweet letter about how he wanted to be a female impersonator and mostly he wanted to impersonate me. So I invited him to the studio to watch me work in *Belle of the Nineties* a couple of years ago. I fascinated him, as I always do. In no time at all, he walked like me, talked like me, sang like me, and finally looked like me. It was a terrific transition. I felt the kid had the stuff to make it real good in drag. But his family was givin' him a lot of trouble. I don't know much about them. He said he had an older brother who said he'd be punished because drag was immoral. Hell, in some places it's even illegal." She laughed. "In a lot of places they're trying to declare *me* illegal. I've even been denounced in the Senate."

"How stupid!" declared Father Riggs.

"Anyway, I had Neon up here for dinner one night and set him straight. I said, 'Neon, you stick to your guns. Follow your star. It's obvious you're meant to live your life in drag and you look so good in them dresses I lifted from Paramount's wardrobe, you make me jealous a little. So anyway, Neon, female impersonatin' might make you rich and famous.' Well, he's takin' it all in eagerly. I tell him about Julian Eltinge, the greatest female impersonator what ever lived besides Queen Christina of Sweden. I knew Julian well back in the old days. He made a fortune. There's a theeyater on Forty-second Street named for him; in fact, I think he built it himself. Take my friend Ray Bourbon, he's never out of work even when he forgets to shave his mustache. The only female impersonator I know who came to a bad end was struck by lightnin' on the Atlantic City pier, but that was because he was out cruisin'. Can't remember his name but he did a great act."

She sauntered slowly to her white fireplace and posed with one hand on the mantel. "Well, I helped get Neon his first booking. It was at the Limp Wrist in Brentwood. He was a sensation. You see, Neon didn't only do me. He did a terrific Garbo. His Katherine Hepburn was a riot. He did a great Dietrich and his legs were better—she's knock-kneed, y'know." She lowered her hand from the mantel and began pacing again. "But then he got into bad company. He needed a manager and some son of a bitch put him onto a rat named Milton Connery."

Jim Mallory said, "Isn't the Tailspin his club?"

Mae responded, "I don't know if he owns it outright or just has a piece of it, but he operates out of there. Christ . . . sorry, Father . . . is he bad news. Among his specialties is organizin' orgies"—she assumed it was the priest who was clucking his tongue—"and all sorts of kinky parties. You boys must have known about this. What about it, Herb?"

"We knew about it but it was so cleverly orchestrated, we couldn't get a thing on Connery. Still can't. But we did get a tip on an orgy going on at Lionel Atwill's house—"

"The actor?" It was a rare moment when Mae West looked amazed. "Good old reliable Lionel gave orgies?"

"I haven't got any figures, Mae, but he gave the one we raided. Collared some big names beside Atwill."

Mae hip-wriggled her way to him. "Come on, come on, give.

18

Names. Names, Villon, names. I gotta keep my girls in the kitchen happy."

"We snared Wallace Beery and Walter Pidgeon for starters."

"I love it! I love it! Say, Father, why ain't they been denounced by the church?"

"Probably because the church didn't know about them. Anyway, we're not interested in what people do in the privacy of their homes."

"What's so private—no pun intended—about orgies?" She returned her attention to Villon. "There's more to them orgies than what meets the eye, right?"

"Of course. There were hidden cameras that took pictures for blackmail. A lot of silver crossed a lot of palms."

Jim Timony got some words in edgewise. "Say, I thought Berry and Pidgeon patronized Polly Adler's whorehouse exclusively!"

"And you oughta know," Mae said with a knowing wink.

Agnes asked sweetly, "Doesn't Polly Adler operate out of New York?"

"Yeah," confirmed Mae, "but she fills mail orders. I never did believe in orgies though I've had my share of invitations. I'm a one-man woman—one at a time, that is. I ain't never been caught in flagrante delicious. Anyway, do you suppose the autopsy on Neon showed he was wastin' away? He got very sick. Look it up, Villon, I'd be interested to know. Poor kid, gettin' his skull crushed in Griffith Park. Say, wait a minute . . . from what I hear that's a pretty busy park, day *and* night. How come there was no witnesses?"

Timony suggested, "Maybe there were."

"Nah," said Mae, waving his suggestion away. "If there'd been a witness, his murderer would have been caught. Right, Villon?"

"Off the top of my head, Mae, it's my guess Neon was murdered somewhere else and his body dumped in Griffith Park."

"That's real sound thinkin'. Which is why you're a detective

19

and I ain't." Hands on hips, her favorite place for them, she spotlighted Timony. "Jim, why'd you book Beverly into the Tailspin?"

"You told me to get her a job, for crying out loud. They had an opening and were glad to have your sister."

"You have a sister?" Agnes was truly astonished.

"Yeah, honey, and someplace there's a brother, John. Not too sure about where he's landed, but Beverly is somethin' else again. You know what she does in her act? She does *me*. She's *another* Mae West impersonator. We're the same size. She wears my castoffs when I'm in the mood to do any castin' off. Oh, Christ—sorry, Father—now she'll be in danger too! Jim, we need to audition some muscle for Beverly too. She likes Eye-talians especially. See if you can find a couple of nice ones. Maybe I'll lend her Steel Cheeks!"

The Indian jumped to his feet and spoke ferociously. "No! I protect you and only you! I will never leave your side!"

Mae wiggled her hips. "Now, ain't that touchin'? He's better then a Labrador retriever and a hell of a lot more fun. Seymour, you're a treasure and I'm glad I dug you up. Leavin' so soon, Father?"

Father Riggs went to her and took her hand. "Yes, I have choir practice in half an hour."

"Oh, yes, choir practice. Is it an all-boy choir?"

"Oh, indeed."

"Oh, yeah? In good deed or bad deed? I'll have to come around some day and give them the once-over, maybe give them a few pernters about life. I'll see if I can fit them into my busy schedule."

"And thank you again for your generous donation."

"Just remember to mention me in your prayers. It looks like I might be needin' all the help I can get."

"I always bless you, Mae."

After he departed, Mae said, "He's too damned gorgeous to hide his light in the confessional. I'm gonna have a talk with Lupe Velez. That nutty Mexican is Catholic, and if anyone can

20

smoke him out, she can. What's botherin' you, Agnes? You got that weird look again."

"It's you, Mae."

"Cut it out. Don't talk like that. You're beginnin' to scare me."

"You need protection, Mae."

"Well, Jim's gettin' it for me, so cut out that mumbo jumbo. If you're all that good a witch, why ain't you castin' a spell of protection over me?" Desdemona entered from the kitchen. "Hey, Desdemona, how's the market in rabbit's feet?"

"Bad for rabbits."

"She makes jokes yet!" Mae exclaimed in exasperation.

"Goneril wants to know how many for lunch."

"Oh, tell her to lay it out on the sideboard buffet style. Anyway, I just lost my appetite to a vampire. And tell Goneril I've had enough of those Aunt Jemima pancakes!"

Desdemona shrugged and left. Herb Villon asked Mae, "Now it's my turn to say a dollar for them."

"It's kind of a crazy notion, but I was suddenly thinkin' about Gladys George."

"Should I know her?"

"If you appreciate good acting, you should. She's a Broadway name out here doing a picture at Paramount. She was the star of *Personal Appearance*, the pitcher I'm doin' now, y'know, *Go West, Young Man*. She wanted to do the pitcher herself and got sore as hell when Paramount said they wanted me to do it. So they offered her *Valiant Is the Word for Carrie*. She took it—a mother role, for cryin' out loud—and now she stares daggers at me every time our paths cross, which gratefully ain't too often. So help me Hannah I tried to convince my producer, Manny Cohen, to give her the damned movie. I never wanted to do it in the first place. I like to write my own stuff. In fact, I had to rewrite this script because there wasn't the real feel of Mae West in it." There was a wicked twinkle in her eyes. "And to be real good you gotta have the real feel of Mae West. Ahhh, they wouldn't let me do Catherine the Great because it's only been a couple of years since Dietrich did hers. So then I says, okay, boys, how's for me doin' Joan of Arc and I seduce the dauphin of France and set myself up in a nunnery which is a front for a house of prostitution? Everybody starts crossin' themselves. Even my producer, and he's Jewish. I knew I couldn't win."

In the kitchen, Desdemona announced, "No more Aunt Jemima pancakes."

"Sheeee-it," roared Goneril, who was actually Desdemona's older sister. "I just bought more stock!"

In the living room, Mae was dismissing Jim Timony, sending him and Seymour Steel Cheeks on their scouting expeditions to the local gymnasiums. "Only first-class contenders, boys, no stumblebums." She watched them leave, then returned her attention to the detectives. "You know, it's not as though I don't have enough to worry about these days. My supportin' players are a bunch of prima donnas. I got Alice Brady from the Broadway Bradys—her father William is a great producer and married to a terrific actress, Grace George. Alice is pretty damn good herself, but now she's doin' supports and she still can't live with it. To think she once had an affair with Clark Gable. Then there's Elizabeth Patterson. Now she's been around since the year one. I like Liz but she keeps tryin' to upstage me. Me! That's like tryin' to move the Empire State Building! I got two leading men. One, Randolph Scott, he's on his way up. Warren William is the other one, and he's on his way down. Randy is cute but not very randy. Randy has a stopwatch and clocks every scene he's in. Acksherly, I like a man who times his takes."

"Seriously, Mae," said Villon, "we'll have to get some protection for your sister too."

"You don't have to worry about that," Mae reassured him. "My protection will be her protection. She'll be stayin' here with me. And let me tell you, if that vampire tries sweepin' into my all-white domain, he'll have two firebrands to contend with. Remember, we were born and brought up in Brooklyn so we know how to hold our own. It was a pretty tough neighborhood but we learned to give as good as we got, which we soon didn't get too often. Our father was Battlin' Jack West."

Jim Mallory came to life. "A prizefighter?" He was a sports nut.

"And what a prizefighter. The only person he couldn't lick was my mother." She paused. "That didn't sound right, did it?" The four enjoyed a good laugh.

Agnes Darwin smothered the mood. "It's still with me. That uneasy feeling is still with me. I shall prepare fetishes for you and Beverly."

"What in the hell are fetishes?"

"They ward off evil. They're a specialty of African witch doctors."

"Well, I ain't goin' to no Africa, much as I like black people."

"You don't have to go anywhere. I can get what I need at the Witches' Brew."

"What's *that?*"

"An occult supermarket on Fairfax Avenue."

"What I need is *real* protection against vampires. A platinum cross around my neck, maybe set with a dozen diamonds or so. I'll have the girls put garlic on all the windows. I'll add more mirrors to the place because vampires don't cast no reflections. And anyway, a girl can't have enough mirrors around." She spoke seductively to Jim Mallory, whom she now realized also had a strong pair of shoulders under his badly fitting jacket. "I like to look at m'self from all sides, especially after I've soaked for a long time in a well-salted bath. And there go them damn chimes again."

Agnes Darwin's stomach growled ferociously. "I need food," she announced to everyone.

"Yeah, yeah," said Mae, waving Agnes back as she started to rise from the couch. "Just as soon as I conclude my next audience."

Desdemona entered and announced, "Rabbi Morris Rothfeld."

Mae smiled and said, "I always offer equal time. I help the

rabbi's synagogue. And besides, my mother was half Jewish. Hello, Rabbi! Come on in! Ain't he gorgeous? He's the youngest rabbi in captivity and ever since I met him I've been doing my damndest to be a rabbi rouser. Don't be so shy, Rabbi, you and Father Riggs have the kind of good looks that should be shared with the world. Come meet my friends! Desdemona! My checkbook, my bottle of ink, and my quill. Rabbi, this is Agnes Darwin, a real, authentic, practicin' witch."

"Delighted to meet you," said Morris Rothfeld, while wondering which witch did her hair.

"And these are my two detective friends, Herb Villon and Jim Mallory." They shook hands. "I'm sure you've been reading about how my impersonators are gettin' themselves murdered."

"I most certainly have." His voice was baritone and imposing. Mae was sure he made the synagogue windows rattle during the Jewish high holidays. "And, Mae, I have brought you protection."

THREE

"WELL, HOW ABOUT THAT!" EXCLAIMED MAE as she led the rabbi to the desk. He fished a small rectangular metal disk from his jacket and held it in the palm of his hand for her to see. "It's so nice to know there are so many good friends interested in my welfare." She examined the metal disk. "What is this thing?"

"It's called a mezuzah. Inside there's a tiny scroll inscribed with biblical verses. They're from Deuteronomy. You nail it to the panel to the right of your door."

"You mean outside in the hall?"

"That's right. Every time you enter your apartment, you kiss your fingers and then press them against the mezuzah. That is for health and for safety."

"Mezuzah, eh? Sounds like a Greek appetizer." She spoke to Mallory. "Hey, good-lookin'. Make yourself useful. Get a hammer from the girls in the kitchen. They're the keepers of the tools. They also got nails. Hammer this here thing in place. I ain't wastin' any time givin' myself protection, right, Rabbi?"

"Right. Just always remember to kiss the mezuzah."

"Somehow I'm thinkin' there's a double intended there." She signed her name to the check with a flourish, placed the quill aside, tore the check from the book, and waved it to dry the ink. "Y'know, Rabbi, I oughta set up a double screen test for you and Father Wally. Y'interested?"

"If it means money for my synagogue, then I'm interested. But I'm not an actor."

"You're one hell of a singer." She said to Agnes and Herb Villon, "Rabbi invited me to a Friday night service and I was happy to attend, even though it meant skippin' the fights. It was a real interestin' experience. I ain't never been inside a synagogue before. I mean, my mother bein' half Jewish didn't mean she was religious. That sort of stuff didn't interest her. She only cared about us kids. Anyway, in this here synagogue I gotta sit upstairs in the balcony with the women, isolated from the men, get it? Rabbi turns me over to his wife, Goldie, right?"

"Goldie is right," said the rabbi. "Goldie is always right, or else."

"Come on now, Rabbi, Goldie's okay. I like her. And let me tell you, Herb and Agnes, out comes Rabbi wearin' his skull cap, a prayer shawl draped around his shoulders, with a choir of a dozen boys for backup. Then he opens his mouth and all of a sudden I'm nervous, like it's his opening night. But then, there came from his mouth the most glorious sounds I have ever heard. And I've heard Caruso and Chaliapin and Lawrence Tibbett, and let me tell you, they don't hold a candelabra to Rabbi here. Why, Rabbi, you're blushin'. Ain't he adorable. And look at those shoulders."

"Mae, please, you're embarrassing me."

"Put this check in your wallet and use some of it to take your wife to the Brown Derby for dinner. Tell me when you want to go and I'll set it up for you."

"Thank you, but we don't go to fancy places like the Brown Derby. They don't serve kosher food."

"So go for some coffee and cake and look at the movie stars. Goldie could use a night out."

They could hear Mallory hammering the mezuzah to the panel.

Mae smiled and said to the rabbi, "I guess that's sweet music to your ears. It's just as sweet to mine. Join us, Rabbi. We're going to have some lunch."

"Thank God," said Agnes as she jumped to her feet. Mae took the rabbi's arm. She was genuinely fond of the young man.

"I've already had my lunch," he lied, "but I'd enjoy some coffee."

"Don't kid me, Rabbi. My food ain't kosher, but I understand. I had a Jewish lover once, and I was crazy about him. But it didn't work out."

"What a shame," said the rabbi. "What went wrong?"

"He had a Jewish mother."

Mallory joined them and smacked his lips at the lavish buffet. "The girls lay a nice spread."

"And they've got the spreads with which to do it," said Mae. "Hey, Rabbi. Here's smoked salmon and smoked whitefish. Real kosher! Don't they fit the bill?"

"They most certainly do," agreed the rabbi. Desdemona and Goneril stood on either side of the sideboard, beaming with pleasure.

"I have to thank you book ends for considering Rabbi might join us for lunch."

Goneril sniffed and said, "I always keep a kosher kitchen."

Mae winked at the rabbi. "Goneril's always cooked for Jews."

"Indeed?" said the rabbi. "How did she come to you?"

"I won her in a crap game."

When all were seated at the dining table, the rabbi lowered his knife and fork and looked at Mae. If only her detractors knew what a truly lovely woman she was. Her physical attributes couldn't hold a candle to her beautiful soul and the warmth of her heart. If they could see the numbers on the check she had written. If at Christmastime and other times of the year they could be there when he and Goldie opened the cartons she sent to the synagogue. Clothes. Shoes. Canned goods for the needy. Cookies for the children. Even movie magazines, especially those that featured her on their covers.

"Rabbi," said Mae, "somethin' wrong with your eyes? They're all misty."

"I'm sorry. I'm a very sentimental person. My wife says when we go to an occasional movie, the minute I hear the opening music, I cry at the credits. But in truth, I was thinking of you and your warmth and your generosity and so many repay you with lip service."

"This here lip service. Is it another double intended?"

"Lip service is insincerity," explained Villon.

"Oh, yeah?" said Mae, picking a bone out of her whitefish. "When I get lip service, honey, it's never insincere." The rabbi laughed. "Look at those teeth, will ya. What about them, Agnes. Pure white and shinin' like spotlights. Now there's a set of teeth I wouldn't mind sinkin' into my neck." The rabbi was blushing again. "Say, Rabbi, you ain't a vampire by any chance, are you?"

"Jews could never be vampires," he replied solemnly. "Although during the many inquisitions we have suffered over the centuries, our people have been accused of drinking the blood of children. And sadly, today, this monstrous myth is being revived and perpetrated in Germany. Tell me, Mr. Villon, like just about everyone else, I've been reading about these awful murders. Is Mae really in danger?"

"As a precaution and for security reasons, we have to look on these killings as a possible threat to Miss West's life."

"Don't be so formal, Herb, call me Mae just like all the cops in my life have called me."

"You like cops?" asked the rabbi with charming ingenuousness.

"Sure I like cops. Most of them are very interestin'." She was smiling at Jim Mallory. "Especially the way they use their nightsticks."

"Now, Mae," admonished Agnes the witch, "enough of your *double entendres*. You're making the fuzz uncomfortable."

"Well, now they know how I feel with this death threat hanging over my head. Up till now, I always thought vampires were a pain in the neck. Now they're starting to drive me bats.

Why isn't Paramount Pictures doin' something about protecting me?"

"They are," Herb Villon comforted her. "I met with their security police this morning and they're on the alert. You'll be well protected."

"I know all the boys in security," said Mae as she stirred a cup of coffee. "I've interviewed each and every one of them personally. Most have recovered. They're a very agreeable bunch except for a few stubborn ones who insist on bein' faithful to their wives. Now tell me, Rabbi, you got any theories on why these killin's?"

"I've got a theory, and then there's Goldie's theory."

"Let's hear Goldie's first."

"Well, she thinks there's a religious fanatic at large."

"I can't think of a vampire being a religious fanatic."

"I don't believe vampires exist," the rabbi said flatly.

Mae shifted in her seat. "Then how do you explain them puncture marks above the jugular?"

"With all due respect to the very competent detectives sitting here, I think they're a red herring."

"They don't sound like any kind of fish to me, no matter what the color."

Agnes had lit a cigarette. "Mae, sweetie, don't you read detective stories?"

"I ain't got no time, don't you know that by now?"

Agnes exhaled a smoke ring and said, "Red herrings are as important to detective stories as tall tales are to a liar. In other words, red herrings are false and misleading clues." She added somewhat pompously, "The expression is of British origin. During fox hunts, a herring would be drawn across the trail to confuse the hounds."

Mae waved the smoke of Agnes's cigarette away from her face and said with irritation, "Now, who would want to pull a dirty trick like that?"

"A fox lover," snapped Agnes, while taking the hint and drowning her cigarette in her cup of coffee.

"Forgive the interruption, Rabbi, but from what my friend

Herb here has told me, the coroner insists those are actual fang marks.''

The rabbi shrugged. "I'm sure there exists some sort of sharp instrument with double prongs that could leave a simulation of fang marks. Or else the instrument could be designed and made by a competent toolsmith. Isn't that possible, Mr. Villon?''

"Anything is possible in a murder case, Rabbi. And I'm open to all suggestions. I like yours a lot. We'll have to look into that idea, Jim. Anyway, Rabbi, it wasn't the bite that killed the victims. Although it drew blood, it was a knife to the heart that finished them off.''

"Then I'm right!'' the rabbi said triumphantly. "If it was really a vampire, he would have sucked his victims dry, give or take a few drops. If this so-called vampire has to use a knife to finish off his victims, then he's just plain *meshuga*.''

Through clenched teeth Mae explained to Agnes, "Which means he's just plain screwy.'' To the rest of the table she declaimed, "Screwy or not, he's dangerous. Not only to me, but to my sister.'' In reply to the confused look on the rabbi's face, Mae told him about her sister, Beverly, and her impending arrival in Hollywood and booking at the Tailspin Club.

"I am told it is positively a den of iniquity,'' said the rabbi, addressing his remarks to Herb Villon. "You should close it.''

"We've got no reason to close it. True, it's a hangout for homosexuals, but it's one of the better bars in town. They serve good food and drinks. The prices are reasonable. They get a well-behaved clientele including a lot of the movie and radio crowd. I've been there myself with my girlfriend. They have great entertainment. The drag acts are a riot. The has-beens who are grateful to get a date there are still good entertainers, and they're truly appreciated and warmly applauded. No, Rabbi, it's not a den of iniquity. It's an oasis where the oddballs can rub elbows with and look after their own. And believe me, Rabbi, lots of single women go there because they know they'll find good company and won't be hassled.''

"Lesbians!'' snapped the rabbi.

"And Lithuanians and Latvians,'' dead-panned Villon, paraphrasing a tired Sam Goldwynism. The apocrypha being that when told Lillian Hellman's play, *The Children's Hour*, which he planned to film, was about a suspicion of lesbianism being practiced by the two female leads, Goldwyn said impatiently, "All right, so we'll change them to Lithuanians!"

"Now listen, Rabbi," counseled Mae, "not all women in gay hangouts are lesbians. Besides, they stick to their own places, like the one in the valley called the Warrior's Husband."

"What about this shady character, Milton Connery? Isn't he supposed to be connected to the Tailspin Club?"

"All of Los Angeles knows about that," said Villon.

Mae leaned forward. "Rabbi, let me give you a little education in shady characters. Will you think any less of me if I tell you most of my shows on Broadway were backed by gangsters? You heard of Owney Madden? Lepke Buchalter? Arnold Rothstein? Frank Costello? To you they were gangsters and still are, to me they were angels. Does associatin' with these guys strictly on a business level make me a shady character?"

"No, my dear Mae, it most certainly does not. And I apologize for being so straitlaced and seeming so narrow-minded. Let alone it's unbecoming in a rabbi, it is unbecoming in anyone."

"Good for you, Rabbi. Let me set you straight about the immediate vicinity. The studios and their unions are up to their ears in mob infiltrators. Right, Herb?"

"Dead right."

"Who knows, maybe one of them has a contract out on me and the assassin is sufferin' from a case of the cutes and decided to lay it all on a vampire. Vampires can't defend themselves because I suppose they ain't got no union. Say, Agnes, do witches have a union?"

"No, dear, we have an association that publishes a monthly newsletter. I do a column, 'Straight from My Broomstick.'"

"That must be a tough balancin' act."

Agnes's voice was deadly. "No, dear, that's the name of my column."

Mae smiled. She enjoyed annoying Agnes. She realized that her maids had been in attendance and on their feet all this while. "Girls, why don't you clear away, have your lunch, and take a siesta. I wonder how Timony and Seymour are makin' out in the gyms. They're both probably tryin' to double cross me, holdin' out for guys with crossed eyes and warts on the tip of their noses. Well, those can always be medically treated. In my time," she said as she sinuously led the way back to the living room, "I've had a lot of medical treats. Say, Herb, I'll be takin' a big table for Beverly's openin' Friday night. Why don't you and Jim join me, I'd be delighted to have you. Bring your girlfriends too."

"I don't have one," Jim Mallory said quickly.

"Why, honey?" asked Mae. "Can't you afford one?"

Herb explained with a sly grin, "Jim doesn't seem to make out with women. He's very shy."

"Of what?"

"The poor man's blushing," said Agnes. "Don't be mean, Mae."

"I ain't bein' mean," Mae said good-naturedly. "Jim's too attractive to be unattached. Why, Jim, if I didn't think Seymour Steel Cheeks would crush every bone in your body and a few more, I'd invite you to be my escort. Anyway, I want you there just the same. The more the merrier. They say there's safety in numbers. Do you suppose they mean the ones from one to ten or those prowlin' around on the scent? Agnes, there's that damned creepy look on your face again."

Agnes was embracing herself, warding off a chill. "I can't help it when these things come over me. Tomorrow's Hallowe'en, All Hallow's Eve."

"Yeah, honey, I know. The night the witches come out to play. Is it a night for kind witches or evil witches?"

"It's a night for all witches. There'll be mischief afoot. There's an open house at all the bars. The big party is at the Tailspin."

"You goin'?"

"Oh, yes. It's de rigueur."

Mae exploded. "There you go again, damn it, with some more of that fancy French footwork of yours!"

Agnes folded her arms and said sternly, "De rigueur has been adopted into our language. Everyone uses it."

"This is the first time I ever heard it!"

"It means that it is expected I be at the party."

"So why the hell don't you say so!" Mae froze in position. A thought struck her. Suddenly she snapped her fingers. "Marie Antoinette!"

"Where did *she* come from?" asked Agnes.

"Austria," the rabbi told her.

Mae was off on a cloud of her own creation. "Marie Antoinette! That's who I'll do next! I can't do Catherine the Great, I'll do Marie Antoinette!"

Herb Villon knew his next words were a calculated risk. "Er, Mae, I think I read in one of the trades that MGM is thinking of Norma Shearer as Marie Antoinette."

The hands were firmly entrenched on the hips. The eyes were narrow, threatening slits. "Shearer couldn't play no queen. She ain't got the class. Even Shirley Temple would do a better job then her. *Me!*" She jabbed her delightful bosom with a carefully manicured thumb. "I'm the queen of queens. When I tell the peasants who are bein' revoltin' to eat cake, I'll even lend them a couple of recipes. I can see myself climbin' the steps to the guillotine, seductively wigglin' my backside. That'll give them somethin' to think about. Then when I get to the scaffold platform, I'll turn to them with a look of defiance. I'll put my hands on my hips like I'm doin' now and maybe sing somethin' like 'Minnie the Moocher' and then a big peasant dance number choreographed by someone like Madame Albertina Rasch. Yeah! Somethin' real snappy. And I go over so great, they decide to spare me and I don't lose my head, except maybe to one of the guards standin' near me if he's gorgeous enough."

"Mae," Agnes said dryly, "you can't screw around with history."

"Agnes, I can do anythin' I damn well please. Hmmm." She was back floating on her cloud. "Now for the dauphin what's my husband, I think I'll insist on Gary Cooper."

"He is physically all wrong," advised Agnes.

"Get your eyes examined, honey. He is physically all right, and how, ummmmm!"

"Mae, I've got to be going," said the rabbi.

"Choir practice?"

"You must be psychic."

"No, all you clergymen use that for an exit line. Father Wally also had to get to choir practice. Well, I've seen *your* choir. They're a little young, even for me. Give Goldie my best and remember, you treat her to a night out. All work and no play make a rabbi's wife a dull girl."

She took his arm, walked him to the door, and opened it. "Hey will you look at my mezuzah! Nice and shiny and protective." She kissed her fingers and touched the mezuzah. "How about that?"

"Very good, Mae. Very very good."

A few minutes later, sitting in the throne chair and contemplating Agnes and the detectives, she announced a decision. "I ain't waitin' till Bev's openin' night. I'm gonna check out the Tailspin tomorrow night."

"It'll be a madhouse," advised Agnes.

"So who told you I was all that sane?" She saw the look on Villon's face and it was a patently disapproving one. "I'll have my bodyguards with me, Herb. And what's more, there's bound to be a lot of Mae Wests there."

Villon said, "There might also be a vampire."

FOUR

THERE MIGHT ALSO BE A VAMPIRE.

After the detectives left, Agnes opened a window that led to a balcony, sat on the sill, and lit a cigarette, directing the smoke to the outdoors. Next to the window were double doors that opened properly onto the balcony, but Mae had yet to furnish the balcony with chairs. Mae West had one thing in common with vampires. She avoided the sun. She liked her skin white and she kept it that way. Los Angeles seemed to always be ablaze with sunlight, and it was frequently ferociously hot and unbearable. On the rare occasion she took a short walk in the daytime, Mae protected herself with an oversized parasol. She also favored garden hats with abnormally wide brims. In defiance of any current fashion, she wore her dresses to the ankle. The spiteful rumor was that this was because she had fat, ugly legs. This was not so. Her legs were shapely, but Mae felt dresses to the ankle gave her stature, especially with the help of her platform shoes.

"One of these days, them cigarettes are gonna do you in like they did my father. Battlin' Jack had a wrackin' cough all his adult life, which wasn't a very long one. I like you, Agnes. I'm glad we're friends. I ain't got many women friends. There's you, there's Beverly when she isn't being a pain in my backside, and there's Desdemona and Goneril."

"How long have they been with you?"

"Ever since I decided to settle out here and make my fortune. I didn't get them through no agency either. I got them through Central Castin'. Central sent over a dozen black ladies to audition to be my maid and my cook. When in walked Desdemona and Goneril lookin' like twins, which they ain't, I knew I had it made. They share a nice apartment on the floor under me. I had a special staircase constructed for them that leads from their kitchen into my kitchen. They're a real comfort to me."

"Don't you have any women acquaintances at Paramount?"

"No, there's nobody there I've taken to. Dietrich is cozy with Claudette Colbert, Miriam Hopkins is cozy with herself, Carole Lombard prefers the fellers and curses like a longshoreman, and Sylvia Sidney cries a lot. I never get too friendly with the women in my pitchers because I think they're all afraid of me. I liked Rafaela Ottiano on *She Done Him Wrong*. She played Russian Rita, but she also did it with me in New York so we had a lot to talk about. She's settled out here too, but she lives with her father and doesn't welcome men's advances."

"She a dyke, maybe?"

"If she is, she's a very quiet one. Sends me Christmas and Easter cards. Nice lady."

"Jim Timony still giving you a hard time?"

"Agnes, nobody gives me a hard time. Anyway, Jim's on the verge of retirement."

"Oh, really? I didn't think he'd ever retire."

"Neither did he. But it's time he went. He's in love with me and I sure ain't with him. I'll give him a good settlement."

"What about Seymour Steel Cheeks?"

"Just a nosh. An interim booking. One day soon he'll move on. They always do. Especially I'm so much older than they are. When the novelty of livin' with Mae West wears out, they move out. And I move on. You got a new man in your life, Agnes?"

"I think I do. He's a warlock."

"Who are the warlocks?"

Agnes flipped the cigarette stub out the window and sat in an easy chair opposite Mae's throne. "Warlocks are male witches."

"Say, listen, spooky. Was all that jazz true about you comin' from a long line of witches?"

Agnes smiled. "It is very very true. Now listen, Mae, do you really think it advisable you go to the party tomorrow night? It'll be bedlam. The boys'll be girls and the girls'll be boys and there's going to be a lot of heavy drinking and it could be dangerous."

"You haven't known real danger until you've faced the New York critics on an openin' night. All kiddin' aside, I've got to get out and see what's doin' in the world. When I'm not locked into shootin' a movie, I'm cooped up here mostly because there's no place to go and if there was, there's nobody to go with. And believe me, Jim Timony is no one to go with. Oh, I go to the fights on Friday nights and then down to Chinatown afterward for some chop suey. Now and then I steer Steel Cheeks to the Mocambo or the Cocoanut Grove, but after half an hour or so of everybody starin' at us, I want to go home and flip pages in a movie magazine. This here vampire is about the most excitement I've had in ages, and I want to make the most of him."

"Just make sure he doesn't make the most of you."

"Agnes, bein' a woman, you've heard of woman's intuition. Well, I've got a pretty good one. When Paramount asked me to come out and do *Night After Night* with Georgie Raft, who's a good pal from the old days, I had an intuition a whole new career was openin' up for me and that I'd become a big movie star. It was a small part and my billin' was rotten, but I wrote my own lines. I wore my own diamonds. And when that hat check girl in my first scene when I enter Georgie's club says to me, 'Goodness, what diamonds!' and I say to her, 'Dearie, goodness had nothin' to do with it.' Well, it tore the house down in every pitcher house across the country and I had it made. Georgie Raft said I stole everythin' but the camera. Paramount gave me a great contract with solo starring billing above the title and the option to write my own scripts. After all,

I wrote all my own plays and I had a lot of hits. I've done all right for myself and for Paramount, even if no thanks to the Legion of Decency now forcin' me to clean up my act I've been slippin' a little. But still I'm makin' money for Zukor and his boys, and my contract's ironclad for another two years. I can always go back to the theeyater, and there isn't a show house in America that wouldn't offer me a small fortune to do personal appearances. Anyway, gettin' back to intuition . . ."

She left the throne chair and positioned herself in front of a mirror that hung above a white table. "Agnes, I'm gonna live a long life. Look at my face. Not a line in it. Pure alabaster. It shows no character but believe me, there's plenty there under the skin. I take good care of myself. My mother made me. She made me write my own material. She was a saint. I lost her too soon and I'm still grievin'." She moved her hand from her head to her waist. "See all this. It's a façade. A false front. Underneath, I'm just a kid cryin' for her mama. Anyway, what I'm gettin' to is this, this here vampire, this phony vampire—"

"There's nothing phoney about those murders," Agnes interjected quickly.

"Oh, yes there is. Them puncture wounds are plenty phony. Father Riggs and the rabbi are right. There ain't no such things as vampires."

"There's a species of bats called vampires."

"Yeah and there are primitive people all over the world drinkin' blood. Well, hospitals give patients blood transfusions, don't they? What's the difference except in hospitals it's inter Venus?"

"Intravenous."

Mae shot her a look. If looks could kill, Agnes would have been a candidate for a mortuary. "I think Villon suspects what I'm up to. I'm settin' myself up."

"You're a fool!"

Mae relished Agnes's anger. "Like hell I am. I'm sayin' Come on, killer, here I am out in the open, yours for the takin'. Come and get it. It's bein' served up to you on a diamond platter. No killer's goin' to make a move in as public a place as a nightclub.

It'll be mobbed and I can guarantee you I'll be the center of attention from the minute I make my grand entrance. And I can guarantee you a very grand entrance."

"You listen to me, Mae West. Stanford White was shot dead in a packed nightclub. A gangster was knifed to death on a dance floor doing a tango with his girlfriend."

"He musta been a rotten dancer."

"Please, Mae! You're crazy to expose yourself to this danger!"

"What danger now?" asked Jim Timony, standing in the doorway. As Agnes told him what Mae was planning to do, Timony advanced slowly into the room, Seymour Steel Cheeks behind him.

"You'll do no such thing," Timony said sternly.

"It's no more dangerous than goin' to Bev's opening or to the studio tomorrow. There's more danger on a sound stage than there is anywhere else. There's plenty of hidin' places from which a killer can strike."

Agnes was upset. She asked Timony, "Is there no reasoning with this woman?"

Timony shrugged.

"Sure there is, honey," Mae said as she sauntered about the room, "ask any number of my old boyfriends. And if you find any number of my old boyfriends, they'll be old, Agnes, they'll be old."

"Can't you ever be serious? You're life's in danger!"

"I am often serious and this won't be the first time my life's been in danger. A couple of years ago I got a kidnap threat. Paramount kept it out of the papers. They didn't want to give anybody else any ideas. Jim got me a small-caliber handgun, which can do an awful lot of damage. It's in my bedroom now, in a dresser drawer gettin' its beauty sleep. Tomorrow night it'll be in my handbag. And I'm one hell of a shot."

Agnes turned to Seymour Steel Cheeks, who, standing with his arms folded, looked like an Academy Award. "Seymour, you talk to her. Maybe she'll listen to you."

"She don't ever listen to me," Seymour said forlornly.

"That's because you ain't got much to say. Now everybody snap out of it. What's with the bodyguards, Jim?"

"You're auditioning about a dozen at Hasseltine's Gym in a couple of hours. Jake Hasseltine's promised me some quality goods."

Mae's face turned dreamy. "Jake Hasseltine? Not old 'One-Two' Hasseltine?"

"It'll please him that you remember him."

"How could I forget him? Let me see . . ." She gazed at the ceiling to stimulate her memory. "Chicago. Back in twenty or twenty-one. He fought 'Glass Jaw' Brogan, I think it was. Knocked him out in one round. Went to a party afterward for him at Collesano's. We were introduced, the eyes connected, the hands connected, and then, ummmm, you can figure what else connected." Agnes couldn't believe her ears. The woman's life was in danger and she reminisced about an ancient conquest! "Jake Hasseltine. Boy, he had one hell of a stiff uppercut."

Timony cut in. "What about tomorrow night?"

"Well, what about it? I'm goin' to the Hallowe'en party at the Tailspin. I'm makin' up a small party. Seymour, the detectives and you're welcome to join us if it won't be too hard on your heart."

"There's nothing wrong with my heart."

Nothing wrong, thought Mae, except that I've splintered it. "Agnes, will you book me a table. Since it's so duhrigguh that you be there, I assume you've got clout with the place."

"I'll get a good table. What time?"

"When do you think the fun will begin?"

"Any time you get there."

Mae smiled. "How's about nine?"

"Nine. You've got it."

Mae settled into an easy chair. "Say, Agnes, your clout at the Tailspin wouldn't by any chance be Milton Connery?"

"He's one contact there."

"You know him a long time?"

"Three, four years maybe."

"He interested in witchcraft?"

"Not until he met me."

Mae smiled. "So you cast a spell over him."

"It was the other way around. He's a rat, but as rats go, he was plenty smooth."

"Oh, yeah? You make it sound like he's been partially misunderstood."

"Spare yourself, Mae. Don't get interested in Milton Connery."

"Now, Agnes, stop tryin' to read between my lines. I got enough on my hands without addin' this here Connery or anybody else to my workshop. What I'm actually gettin' at, Agnes, is bein' how you go back three or four years with the bum, then you must have met Neon Light."

"I met him." Her voice was flat, unmelodic. Mae didn't recognize it.

Mae crossed her legs. "Did you just meet him casually or did you get to know him?"

"Nobody got close to him except for Milton, and even that wasn't what I would call close."

"Tell me about Neon."

"Well, you knew him too. What's there for me to tell?"

"For cryin' out loud, what's for you to tell is how did he seem to you. Did he loosen up on his background? He never did with me so maybe he did with you. When people talk about a mutual acquaintance, you get to learn about the person from different angles. I suppose that's how it works when you're doin' detective work."

"For Pete's sake!" Agnes said to Timony and Seymour. "Now she's playing detective!"

Mae's eyes smoldered. "I ain't playin'. This is the real thing. I thought of askin' if you knew Neon when the detectives were here because I figured if it was duhrigguh for you to be at the party tomorrow night, it was a long shot you knew Connery and since he was messed up with Neon Light then you'd have met Neon too. I just decided to wait and do my own cross-examinin' as I'm gettin' real interested in detectives. And the good Lord knows, I've known a small army of detectives in my time."

"Amen to that," said Timony.

"I don't need no help from the second balcony," cautioned Mae. "Okay, Agnes, spill."

"Spill what? I never spent much time alone with the boy. The few times we were out together it was with Milton, and all they did was talk about drag and getting Neon into the big time."

"Did Milton know the kid was sick?"

"He never said anything to me if he did know."

"Did you know?"

"No, I didn't know. What was it?"

"You name it. He had it. Top of the list was cancer, second in position was consumption. He might have also had a hang-nail, but that sorta thing never interested me. It's why he was killed that interests me. Why kill a dyin' man?"

"Maybe his murderer didn't know he was dying."

"Maybe his murderer wasn't takin' any chances. Neon wasn't dyin' soon enough. Neon knew a lot of things the police might be interested in bein' in on. Like things about orgies and hidden cameras and blackmail. Y'know drag queens are shrewd, but they ain't clever. And they talk too much, espe-cially to each other. And too often what they learn they pass on to their johns, and that could get dangerous." She took a moment to address Timony and Seymour. "If I'm keepin' you gentlemen from anything until it's time to go to Hasseltine's," she said regally, "you may take your leave."

Timony remonstrated, "For cryin' out loud, Mae!"

"Beat it."

Timony clenched his fists. The kettle was about to boil over, but Timony knew better than to explode. She always bested him in an argument. He turned and, with as much dignity as he could muster, he walked out of the room. Seymour waited until Timony was out of earshot.

"What's on your mind?" Mae asked impatiently.

"Don't you like Mr. Timony anymore?" He sounded like a

child suspicious of and fearing that his parents were contemplating divorce.

Mae shot a heaven-help-me look at the ceiling and then managed a sort of a smile for Seymour. "I'm a little exasperated these days, Seymour, what with these here murders and me feelin' there's a small army of undertakers rubbin' their palms together at the prospect of winnin' the job of embalmin' me." She refrained from adding there was a large army of women who thought she had already been embalmed. "And anyway, Seymour, us girls don't really like any guys around when we're havin' our private"—she cocked her head toward Agnes—"tettertet." Agnes choked on some cigarette smoke. "You understand, don't you, honey?"

"Sure, Mae. I don't need no mountain to fall on me."

"Oh, well, let's hope one doesn't. Not that there are any in the neighborhood."

She watched him go and then returned her attention to Agnes, who was recovering from her choking attack at the open doors leading to the balcony. "How's for some tea?" Without waiting for an answer, she crossed to the hall leading to the kitchen and shouted for the tea. Agnes watched her and was thinking, Here's one gal who's got it all wrapped up in one package: smart, shrewd, and clever. She was wide open and she was all woman, but she laid it on the line and drove a hard bargain. If this was supposed to be a man's world, then she challenged that. She didn't need a manager anymore, she needed a good lawyer and a good accountant. She was her own manager. Timony had been reduced to a figurehead, and much as he once tried to fight it, he knew he was no longer needed and his days were numbered. They'd been friends an impressive number of years. Disloyalty held no place in Mae's vocabulary. Soon she planned to level with him. She knew he would bow out gracefully, handsomely rewarded. In Hollywood, Jim was a fish out of water, Mae's unneeded satellite. He was a throwback to honkytonks, vaudeville, the raucous Broadway theater of the '20s. Now only Broadway survived, and by the skin of its teeth. Movies were king, and a cruel and demanding tyrant. Mae knew how to handle it, Timony didn't.

She said to Agnes, "There goes that weird look on your face again. What's it mean this time?"

"It means I think you should leave detective work to detectives."

"Do my questions frighten you, Agnes? I thought witches were fearless, like Hollywood agents."

"They don't frighten me because they've been simple enough. Yes, I've known Milt Connery a few years and so I got to meet Neon Light. Yes, I know the Tailspin's a hotbed of orgies and blackmail and God knows what else, but up front the place is as clean as a whistle. As your friend Herb Villon eulogized, it sounds even cleaner. I can't tell you what goes on behind the scenes because I haven't been behind the scenes. As for Neon Light's murder, it's tragic just like the other murders. I didn't know he was seriously ill. He was always popping his pills and taking his own temperature, but I thought he was a hypochondriac."

"How come you never volunteered you knew Connery a couple of years back?"

"It's nothing worth crowing about. How many shady characters do you know that you've yet to admit knowing?"

Mae smiled. "You heard me drop a few for the rabbi. I'll bet he didn't recognize any of them names. You got no idea who might have killed Neon? No suspicion?"

"No, Mae, I don't. Neon didn't interest me. Nor do drag queens in general or female impersonators. To tell you the truth, they make me feel sad. They're neither here nor there. Neither men nor women. I think they live in a twilight world of unreality and they're acceptable only to each other. They love you because you're larger then life, your own androgenous self-invention—"

"Andro . . . *what?*"

"Androgenous. Suggestive of both men and women."

"Ah, come off it. That's Dietrich you're talkin' about. She

44

likes to wear pants. I tried it once and I looked like two packages of unshelled peanuts."

Desdemona wheeled the tea cart into the room. Mae told her to place it between two easy chairs. "Muffins," said Mae.

"Scones," corrected Desdemona.

Hands on hips, Mae exploded. "Christ, but I'm gettin' an education today!"

FIVE

HERB VILLON'S GIRLFRIEND, HAZEL DICKSON, sat across from him in his small office. Herb was on the phone talking to Mae, and Hazel, who made her living peddling gossip to columnists and various other forms of clients who rewarded her hand-somely, was eager to know if he was hearing anything that she could use for a profit. She heard Herb saying to Mae "She's delighted to join you for your sister's opening night but I don't know about tomorrow night. Thursdays she usually practices knife throwing with the other gossip hounds."

"Very funny," muttered Hazel.

"Miss West has a table tomorrow night at the Tailspin. It's Halloween."

"How much Tailspin can we take?" She thought a moment. "On the other hand, there'll be a lot of Hollywood there letting their hair down and regretting it the next morning. And per-haps I can get a little chummy with Mae. She's always turned me down for an interview. Sure, why not."

"Okay, Mae," he said into the phone, "we'll be there at nine. Oh, I'm sure Jim would love it. What? Sure I'll tell him. While he's protecting you, you'll be protecting him. See you tomor-row night." As he replaced the phone in its cradle, he said to Hazel, "I wouldn't count on getting too chummy with Mae West."

46

"Why not? Isn't she friendly?"

"She's friendly, all right. But to a point. I don't think she has many women friends."

"You're right. She doesn't. There's this Agnes Darwin you met today. The witch. Boy, if that isn't a laugh."

"Come to think of it, Hazel, what do witches do for a living?"

"Search me. What are witches supposed to do for a living?"

"I don't know, that's why I'm asking you. You profess to know everything about everything and everybody."

"Don't be sarcastic, it's unbecoming." She examined her fingernails while thinking. "I suppose they're paid to concoct love potions for the lovelorn, cast spells over people who are proving irksome to other people, or give lectures to women's clubs." Hazel scratched her chin. "Mae's obviously good to her sister. And to the hired help."

"Desdemona and Goneril worship her. What about this Jim Timony, her so-called manager?"

"He's been around a long, long time but I hear tell she's beginning to think a long, long time has been much too long. What about the muscle boy?"

"Seymour Steel Cheeks?" Villon laughed. "He's like a puppy dog."

"I've seen his picture. I should have such a puppy dog."

"Tell me, Hazel, got any theories on these vampire killings?"

"It's plain as the nose on your face. All bloodstained roads lead to Mae West."

Villon sighed. "The majority rules, I guess."

Hazel thought he looked tired. They'd been together, give or take a few arguments and subsequent short silences, for almost a decade. Theirs wasn't a passionate relationship. They were in fact more like a childless couple who had their own professions to follow and every so often got together under covers just to keep the franchise. Both admitted to each other they dreaded the thought of ever living with another person and were glad to agree on keeping the status very quo.

Hazel asked, "Do you suppose our Mr. Timony might be behind these murders?"

47

"He's too bulky."

"Now what does *that* mean?"

Villon was familiar with Hazel's tones of exasperation. "He's too clumsy to have committed these killings. This murderer is quick on his feet. He's damned fast. He creeps up on them. He slashes their throats and seconds later he's plunged a knife into the heart. This kind of choreography calls for fancy footwork."

"You think Fred Astaire did it?"

Villon smiled. "You might be close, you know. Someone lithe. Athletic. Young. Twenties to forties."

"What about this Neon Light, heaven help me? No vampire bite. No knife to the heart." She slumped in her chair. "I don't envy a detective's job."

"Me either. Neon's only link to the three others is that he impersonated Mae among others. I've got Jim looking up the files on the case right now. Neon's manager was Milt Connery, and he functions out of the Tailspin."

"Oh, good. All the more reason to go two nights in a row. Maybe he'll get chummy with me."

"I wouldn't mind that."

"Trying to get rid of me?"

"Trying to get rid of him. He's a bad boy, and Mae just told me on the phone that he and Agnes the witch seemed to have had it off a few years ago."

"Oh, I'm so glad witches have sex. I do so worry about them. I mean, it would be so dull just cruising around on a broomstick especially in a rainstorm and then come home to a nice hot black cat and a kettle stewing with all sorts of offensive ingredients."

"Agnes Darwin is quite a striking-looking woman. She should shoot her hairdresser, though."

"Is she lithe? Athletic? Young? Twenties to forties?"

"She smokes too much."

"Then she probably gets winded easily. Anyway, why would she want to murder West impersonators?"

"Search me. I don't even know why the murderer wants to

murder them. All I know is, three's a crowd, and I'm not looking forward to any more victims."

"You said three's a crowd. What about Neon Light?"

"I just have a hunch somebody else killed him. The body was found in Griffith Park, but you find all sorts of queer things in Griffith Park."

"Especially queers."

"No, Neon Light was murdered elsewhere and then dumped in the Park at a safe hour in the middle of the night. The only real thing he had in common with the others was his profession. I do strongly feel there could be some other link, but it's going to take a lot of digging to find out what it is."

"You think Milton Connery is some kind of link?"

"All the victims have appeared as headliners at the Tailspin at one time or another. You know, female impersonators and drag acts are limited in bookings unless they're headliners, and there hasn't been a genuine headliner in years. They get booked around the country in small venues. Mostly homosexual bars and clubs and occasionally sleazy joints that still offer some form of vaudeville. Some of them get lucky and are booked into Europe. They go over big in Germany and in Paris. Germany's been an oasis for female impersonators for years. Also North Africa." Hazel was engrossed. "Tunisia, Tangier, Egypt. It's a big market for them. And let's not forget the greatest haven for female impersonators is in the Far East. Japan's Kabuki theater and the Chinese opera. Strictly female impersonators."

Hazel sat up in her chair. "Herbert Villon, how come you know so much about them?"

"What the hell do you mean? I've been reading up on them. Research. If I'm trailing somebody killing female impersonators, then I've got to find out all I can about female impersonators."

"You know there's a rumor around that Mae West is really a man?"

"Hazel, take it from me, she's all woman and a lot of yards wide." He was staring out the window into an alley littered with cartons and garbage cans in one of which a striped alley cat was foraging. "I still keep going back to Milton Connery."

"Have you ever met him?"

"Our paths have crossed, but our swords haven't." He turned in his chair and faced Hazel. "Try to get chummy with him."

"If there's an opportunity, I'll try. I'm not exactly an accredited card-carrying femme fatale." She favored him with a winsome smile. "There are those, on the other hand, who have been known to succumb to my charms, if only briefly. Say, we're not supposed to be going in costume tomorrow night, are we?"

"I don't really suppose so. But if I'm asked what I'm supposed to be, I'll tell them I'm a detective."

"What time tomorrow night?"

"Nine. I'll pick you up a quarter to."

"Now what have I got to wear that's seductive?"

"Wear your enchanting smile. The one you use on the landlord when you're late with the rent."

She shot him a look and then said, "Maybe I'll put a chip of chocolate in my navel and go as a Toll House cookie."

There was a knock on the door and Jim Mallory entered empty-handed. "Neon Light's file is somewhere down in the basement."

"What's it doing down there?" Herb asked, annoyed.

"The clerk said it was getting overcrowded up here so case files they figured unsolvable were moved downstairs."

Herb slammed a hand down on the desk and Hazel yelped. "Who the hell's the clerk to decide a case is unsolvable? Just because it's been up a dead end the past six months doesn't mean there couldn't be a break." He thought for a moment. "Do you suppose somebody asked the file be put in an icebox?"

"I've been entertaining that thought myself. Anyway, he's digging around for it and thinks he might find it in a couple of days or so."

"Why so long?"

"Herb, how long's it been since you paid a visit to the basement?"

"Back in the days when the toilets were down there."

"It has changed. You wouldn't recognize it. And that's because there are floor-to-ceiling packing boxes jammed together, of course alphabetically."

"Very clever idea," Villon offered glumly. He told Mallory about Mae's invitation to the Halloween frolic at the Tailspin. Mallory's face responded like the sun rising in the east.

"Are we supposed to wear costumes? It's awful short notice."

"I don't think it's expected of us elderly folk."

Hazel stared daggers. "I am a long, long way from elderly."

"Now, Hazel," said Villon with a wink to Mallory, "didn't you once tell me you marched with the suffragettes?" He ducked swiftly as a lead pencil went sailing over his head and struck the wall behind him.

With Seymour Steel Cheeks behind the wheel, Mae's limousine pulled up in front of Jake Hasseltine's gymnasium on Santa Monica Boulevard in West Hollywood. It was a three-story brick building surrounded on one side by an empty lot overgrown with weeds and littered with trash and on the other side by a tacky-looking luncheonette known to the locals as the Ptomaine Pit. Seymour hurried around to the back door on Mae's side and opened it for her. She extended her hand and he helped her out. Timony got himself out on the opposite side. He surveyed the rundown neighborhood and thought, If I knew real estate I could buy these parcels up and build and develop and make a handsome profit. But he didn't know real estate and wasn't about to find out about it. He knew he'd soon be heading back East—back to civilization, as he frequently referred to New York—and he was beginning to look forward to it. Looking forward to it despite the three thousand miles that would separate him from Mae. He didn't have to remind himself that now there was more than three thousand miles separating him from Mae. He heard her speaking to him.

"You lead the way in, Jim. And to be on the safe side, just in case Jake ain't the same Jake I knew back in Chicago, you pernt him out to me." Then she added, "But don't be obvious. I don't want to hurt his feelings."

Seymour preceded them to the entrance and held open the unusually large steel door. Mae commented, "Is this a gym or a fortress? I ain't seen a door that size since I served my time on Welfare Island." There was an oversize cement step at the entrance. Realizing she couldn't maneuver it wearing platform shoes, Mae asked Timony to help her up. He put his hand under her elbow and realized it was their first physical contact in over a year. Once inside, Mae groaned. There was a long flight of stairs leading up to the gym. "For cryin' out loud, ain't he heard of escalators?" She said to Timony, "Why didn't you tell me we were goin' mountain climbin'?"

"I suppose I could have told the boys to come to the apartment, but you don't like people to know where you live."

"People, yes, men, no." She took a grip on the handrail and hoisted herself up. "Seymour, you climb behind me in case I lose my grip and start to fall. On the other hand, keep your distance upstairs when I'm interviewin' should I lose my grip and start to fall."

As she ascended the staircase slowly, she heard sounds of her childhood when her mother took her and her siblings to the gymnasium where her father, Battlin' Jack, trained. A wave of nostalgia overtook her and, with it, a tinge of sadness. She could hear gloved fists connecting with punching bags. She heard the nimble footwork of an athlete jumping rope. The familiar sounds of two fighters in a sparring match made her wonder if she looked to her right, would her mother be there warning her there might be blood and not to throw up. Mae never threw up. The sight of the blood excited her, but there wasn't blood too often. Sometimes a sparring mate got carried away and threw one at an opponent's mouth, loosening a few teeth, but that didn't happen too often. She reached the top of the staircase and paused to compose herself. Seymour and Timony knew the routine and waited while she checked herself in a floor-length mirror conveniently nailed into the wall on her left. She knew that future prizefighters liked to pose in front of the mirror with fists poised for imaginary action, a snarl on their lips, heads lifted high, waiting for an imaginary bell to ring and send them into action. They were the modern counterparts of ancient gladiators, soon to go into the arena and face the challenge. *We who are about to die salute you.* Hail, Caesar.

Mae West always enjoyed her reflection in a mirror. She was no great beauty, but she was one of a kind. She had invented herself and owned the patent and would never sell it. The picture hat was just right. The dress had a simple flower pattern. The girdle she wore under it had been especially designed for her so that it gave her a figure what Nature had not seen fit to provide. She was constantly fighting the battle of the bulge, which is why she favored stories that required period costumes rather than modern dress. *Go West, Young Man* was modern, and dress designer Travis Banton almost had a nervous breakdown satisfying the demanding Mae West. There was a simple strand of pearls around her neck and on eight fingers there were a blinding assortment of sparkling diamonds. Her wrists were decorated with six exquisite jeweled bracelets, three to a wrist. It was a miracle that she had never suffered a robbery or been waylaid by bandits when out in public. She was indeed a darling of the gods.

"Let's go in, boys. Jim, you first. Seymour, you follow him and stay a few feet in front of me. Let's not crowd each other."

After Mae made her entrance, there was a gradual diminishing of noise. It was as though every man in the gymnasium was being mesmerized in a mass hypnosis by a master magician. And the smile on Mae's face was indeed magical. At that moment, she heard a tremendous clap of thunder. It was applause. Boxers had removed their gloves to join trainers and handlers in paying tribute to their dream woman. Mae fought back tears, she was so completely taken by surprise. She raised her right hand and gave a perfect imitation of Queen Mary of England standing on a palace balcony acknowledging a tribute from her subjects in the street below.

And then she saw him. Jake Hasseltine. He stood in the center of the ring where he'd been supervising a sparring match between two aspirants who looked as though they were barely out of their teens. Hasseltine wore a T-shirt on which was boldly lettered THE CHAMP. He wore black gym shorts and also sported a black patch over his left eye. Mae lowered her hand and watched as he climbed out of the ring, a wonderful smile that displayed a set of strong but crooked teeth, hands outstretched as though he expected her to run to him. Fat chance. Mae ran to no one. They ran to her, walked to her, crawled to her, especially when drunk. Her professional eye examined him minutely. The arms were still muscular, the stomach was still flat—a hell of a lot flatter than her own—the legs were as sturdy as ever, and the nose, which had been broken too many times to keep count, was an imposing one. Happily, the ears showed no sign of cauliflower.

"I gotta give you a hug, baby, I just gotta."

"You better, you big lug, or I'll jiggle your jewels with my fist."

Timony watched with a set look on his face as they embraced. Seymour Steel Cheeks was perplexed. She once found this old man attractive and sexy? Hasseltine was now in his early forties and in better shape then most men half his age. Seymour was hard put to realize that fifteen or sixteen years earlier, Jake Hasseltine looked like a bronzed Adonis.

Hasseltine's voice was his autobiography. Born on the Lower East Side of Manhattan where he first learned to exercise his fists in order to survive, where he worked alongside his parents and his brothers behind a pushcart on Delancey Street offering a fine array of fresh, and frequently not so fresh, fish for sale. He was a born battler, and his rise to the top in fisticuffs was rapid, almost as rapid as the descent of his star.

"Mae, I seen every one of your pitchers."

"Oh, yeah? There ain't been that many."

"That's okay. I seen them all ten times."

"Ten times? Hmmm. To build up an immunity?"

"Still kiddin' around." He took her arm. "I got some java

and sinkers set up. Thought we'd chin a little before I bring out the boys."

"You sure know how to whet my appetite. Where are the boys?"

"They're upstairs practicin' lookin' tough."

"I ain't climbin' no more stairs!"

"Don't worry, babe. They'll be troopin' down here when I send for them."

Jake led them into his office. On his desk was a pot of coffee on a burner and a plate of small doughnuts. He said with pride, somewhat shyly, "I even got paper napkins, sugar, and milk."

"I hope you got spoons."

Jake guffawed. "Ain't she a kidder? Still kiddin' around, that's my Mae. Sit over here behind my desk, Mae. I bought a new cushion just for you."

"Now, ain't you thoughtful." She sat and emitted an exaggerated sigh. "Ohhhh, ain't that nice and comfortable. Just like you."

"Ahhh, you can't remember all that far back," he said with a grin as he poured coffee for the four of them.

"Oh, no? Why, Jake, I still remember where you've got that mole."

"Ah, cut it out, babe, yer embarrassin' me!"

She said to Timony and Seymour, "Help yourself to the refreshments, boys, and tell me if they're safe. No milk, no sugar for me. I take it black."

"I ain't forgot that, babe." He sat on a wooden chair next to her. "Say, listen, what's goin' on with all these impersonators of you gettin' murdered?"

"That's just what's going' on, Jake. They're gettin' murdered. Seems like there's a local Jack the Ripper out there warmin' up for the big time, meanin' killin' me."

"No way!" remonstrated Jake.

"Any way," said Mae. She had a wicked thought and was delighted to express it. "It couldn't by any chance be a Jake the Ripper, could it?"

"Huh?" Then he grinned. "Still the kidder! That's my Mae!

Always kiddin'!" He dunked a doughnut in his coffee and bit off a chunk. As he chewed he talked and resembled a cement mixer in action. "Ain't the cops got no leads?"

"No leads, no nothin'. Except that maybe there's a vampire out there lustin' for me." She told him about the puncture wounds above the jugular veins.

Awed, Jake shook his head from side to side. "Just like in the pitchers. Hey! Maybe it's just a publicity stunt."

"If it is, it's a pretty sick one." She nibbled daintily at a doughnut. It proved to be amazingly good, crisp on the outside and soft on the inside. "Say, these doughnuts are pretty good. Where'd you get them?"

Jake said with pride, "You see that six-footer jumpin' rope, the one that looks like a station wagon? He makes 'em. He's a great baker. He's hopin' to make enough money fightin' to open a chain of doughnut shops."

"Ummmm, I might consider backin' him myself."

"Listen, Mae," said Jake, suddenly serious, "I know you're here to pick up some bodyguards, but if there's anything I can do . . . I pack a rod and the fists are still two slabs of granite. I can give you great protection."

"That's sweet, Jake, real sweet. But I wouldn't dream of separatin' you from your gym. Anyway, I got some other protection. I got a priest prayin' for me and today a rabbi gave me a mezuzah."

"What's that?"

Mae explained it to him, at the conclusion of which she said, "One of these nights, why don'tcha come up and kiss my mezuzah?"

SIX

FIFTEEN MINUTES LATER, TEN MUSCULAR YOUNG men were lined up for Mae West's inspection. Mae whispered to Jake, "Maybe you better get rid of one or two of them. I had a pretty rough night last night."

Jake looked startled and then he roared with laughter. "Always the kidder! Ha-ha-ha! What a kidder!" He said to the line-up, "You gotta watch out for this gal, fellers. She's always kiddin'."

"Not always, boys. Every so often I get serious and then it's every man for himself, and every other man for me." She sauntered up to the first young man in the lineup. "Young man, your tongue's hangin' out." He shut his mouth fast. "What's your name?" He mumbled. She smiled. "The cat got your tongue, or are you just glad to meet me?"

He swallowed hard and raised his voice a decibel. "Salvatore."

"Salvatore, eh. Like in San Salvatore?"

"No, Miss West. Salvatore Puccini."

"Puccini, eh. It's got a nice lyrical sound. Did you know there was a Puccini who wrote some real cute operas?"

"Yes, Miss West. My pop's got some records. He plays them all the time."

57

"Ohhh? Well that's somethin' your pop and me got in common. I love grand opera. The grander the better. One of these days I'm plannin' to sing grand opera, and I can promise you I'll be real grand. In fact, I'm thinkin' of startin' with *Madame Butterfly*. Of course they'll have to make a few changes to accommodate me. Y'know, in the last act she commits harry carey. You know what that is?"

"Yeah, he acts in the movies."

Mae was stumped, but only momentarily. "It means committin' suicide by stickin' a knife in your stomach and twistin' it until you get nauseous and die. How old are you, Salvatore?"

"Twenty-three."

"Oh, yeah? There ain't nobody that young anymore. Do you think you could do a good job protectin' me, Salvatore?"

"Miss West," he said with the deepest sincerity, "I'd give my life for you."

She turned to Timony, who stood to one side with Jake and Seymour. "You hear that, boys, how's that for generosity?" She returned to Salvatore. "You won't have to go that far, Salvatore." She eyed him again from head to crotch. "You may have to go some kind of distance, but not all that far, if you know what I mean. Jim? You takin' notes?"

"I'm not missing a thing, Mae."

"I didn't think you was. Well, if it's all in your head which I assume since you ain't holdin' no pencil and paper, put a nice check mark next to Salvatore Puccini."

She chatted with three more and then found herself in front of a big black man who towered above her, arms folded and a smile that could have lit up Beverly Hills. "Well, well, well. What have we got here? Looks like your muscles have muscles. What's your name, big boy?"

"Selma." He didn't stop grinning.

"Selma! That's a girl's name. You puttin' me on?"

"No, ma'am. I'm Selma Hamilton Burr. I was born in Selma, Alabama, and my mama promised herself she'd one day have a girl and name her Selma. Well, I'm the ninth son, and Mama was just too plumb tired to go any further so she named me

Selma and that's why I had to learn to use my fists." He laughed. "Can you imagine how many times I had to defend myself when some kid asked me my name and I told him? Anyway, everybody calls me Sel for short."

"Oh, I could never see me sellin' you short, Sel. You're sure one big hunk of man. How old are you?"

"How old do you think?"

"Now, don't be coy. You know with colored people it's always hard to tell their ages until they're white-haired and stooped. I got two great colored gals workin' for me now . . ."

"Oh, yeah?" His eyes lit up with anticipation.

"And I've yet to figure how old they are. As a matter of fact, from day to day they range in age from twenty to thirty-five. So you're Selma Hamilton Burr. What's the Hamilton for, some granddaddy of yours?"

"Oh no, ma'am. Ain't you heard of Alexander Hamilton?"

"Sure I have. I got his picture on a lot of bank notes."

"Then you know that Alexander Hamilton had this here duel with Aaron Burr way back a ways, and my daddy insists we's descended from Aaron Burr so that's how come I'm Selma Hamilton Burr."

"Wasn't Aaron Burr a white man?"

"Yes, ma'am. But my daddy said he fooled around a lot."

"Sel, do you think you could do a good job of protectin' me?"

"Ma'am, do you think anyone could harm you with me surrounding you?"

She laughed. "Yeah, I'll bet you could surround me, and without touchin' me. I'd ask about your eight brothers but I got enough appetite as it is. Jim! Put a check mark next to Selma Hamilton Burr."

She continued along, a general reviewing her troops. How eager these young men were, how blissfully young. There indeed was one with a wart at the end of his nose, but that wasn't a mark against him. It was his buck teeth. They made Mae think of vampires, and Mae had enough to think about on the subject of vampires. She came to the last man on the line. He had blazing red hair and his face was dotted with freckles, but his physique, in Mae's own words, "is a masterpiece." There was no mistaking the insouciance in her voice as she spoke to him. "Do you know your hair's on fire?"

He stood with his hands clasped behind his back. His lips formed into something that might be taken as a smile. "Yeah," he said in a voice that hinted at culture and education, "you want to put out the fire?"

Mae said, "Sure, if you supply the hose." Her eyes covered him from hair to crotch and back up again. "Been trainin' long?"

"I'm not interested in pugilism."

"You ain't? Then what are you doin' here?"

"I work out here. I keep in trim."

"You sure do. So what do you do?"

"I'm a female impersonator."

"Say, kid, you kiddin' me?"

"I rarely kid around. I'm a female impersonator. Right now I'm on the bill at the Limp Wrist. You heard of it?"

"I've heard of everything and a lot of things I wish I'd never heard about. You any good?"

He said in an amazingly accurate imitation of Mae's voice, "Then you know the Limp Wrist is in the valley. Why don't-cha come down and see me sometime?"

Mae laughed. "That's pretty good. Wasn't that pretty good, men?"

Timony said, "It's perfect. The best I've ever heard."

Mae said to the redhead, "Comin' from him, that's a real compliment, and he ain't quick with the compliments. If you're workin' the Limp Wrist, how can you possibly work for me?"

"Miss West, I am so bloody fed up parading around in drag knowing my impressions are giving the wrong impression that I'd kill to get into something else that isn't trimmed in monkey fur."

"Okay, carrot top, what's your name?"

"Dudley Van Helsing."

"Where you from, Dudley?"

"I was born in London. My family's originally from Transylvania."

Timony spoke up. "Transylvania? Isn't that the home of Count Dracula, the vampire?"

"Well, sir, Count Dracula is Bram Stoker's character in his book *Dracula*. The real Transylvanian vampire on whom Stoker based his character was called Vlad the Impaler."

Mae interjected, "Vlad the Impaler. Sounds real interestin', especially the impaler part."

"Actually," said Dudley, "Vlad wasn't really a vampire, though he did murder a slew of men, women, and children and was said to have drunk their blood. Vlad was eventually murdered, but he stayed dead."

"That was mighty thoughtful of him," said Mae. "I wish the one that's after my neck would jern him."

Timony spoke again. "Your surname—Van Helsing. That's the name of the professor in *Dracula* who drives the stake through the vampire's heart."

Dudley smiled. "Sir, my family were actors. Bram Stoker was a theater manager. He was a good friend of my grandfather, Aubrey Van Helsing. He used Van Helsing in his book to please my grandfather, and I'm sure it did."

Mae said, "Why, Jim, I'm pleasantly surprised you know so much about this here book."

"I've had a lot of time to read lately." Mae got his message. "And since we're mixed up with a possible vampire, I decided to do some reading about them."

"Well, we'll have to find some time for you to tell me more. Well, Dudley, are you interested in guarding my body?"

Unsubtly he said, "Very interested."

"You came out here to be an actor, am I right?"

"They tested me at MGM."

"It didn't work?"

"It could have worked, but I prefer to sleep alone in my own bed."

"Smart. Very smart. You get that kind of a reputation in this town and you're finished forever. You also don't get much sleep. How old are you?"

"Twenty-five."

"I need my bodyguards to go to work right away. What do you do about the Limp Wrist?"

"I phone and tell them I've got a better offer. Drive over and collect what they owe me, pick up my costumes, and report for work wherever you want me."

"Ummmm, I want you, all right. Jim! Put a check mark next to Dudley Van Helsing. Okay, it's Puccini, Selma, and Van Helsing. The rest of you gentlemen, I want to thank you for your patience and your cooperation. I ain't never seen so many gorgeous hunks under one roof. Some nights when my insomnia intrudes, instead of countin' sheep, I'll count you gentlemen jumpin' over my bed. And who knows, maybe someday our paths will cross again." She sauntered over to Timony. "You take care of what I pay them. Give them a fair shake. These jobs are gonna be dangerous and exhaustin'. When it's all over and they all survive, I may have to take them on a rehabilitatin' cruise to Hawaii on a chartered yacht. Seymour, do you have to look so sullen?"

"You don't need these musclebound body builders!"

"Says you."

"I am all the protection you need!"

"What's the matter Seymour, ain't you heard 'Variety is the spice of life'?" She sauntered away from him slowly. "Well, I'm always interested in variety, and I always need a lot of spice. Well, Jake, you handsome beast, you are a great talent scout. You approve of my cherces?"

"I couldn't have done better for you myself, Mae. Say, Mae, you know, for old times' sake, maybe we could . . . you know . . . get together again sometime?"

"Why, sure, you hesitant brute. Didn't I invite you up sometime to kiss my mezuzah? I better not invite up too many, it could be unsanitary. Say, Jim! Ain't I got an empty apartment on the floor below me next to the girls' apartment?"

"It's a one-bedroom."

"That'll do fine. Fix it up for the boys." She said to her three new employees, "Boys, you'll be required to sleep on the premises in an apartment under mine so should you hear me screamin', you only have to run up the stairs, break down the door, and put me into a good frame of mind. I'm sure you'll like the arrangement. My cook Goneril will take great care of you. Her sister Desdemona is my personal maid. They're great gals. I know you'll like them." She winked at Selma, who flashed his smile, reminding her of a lighthouse. She said to Timony, "I should let Herb Villon know I've hired these boys."

"It might be a good idea to have him do a check on them," suggested Timony.

"My intuition is all the check we need. These boys are just what I need. I'm also thinkin' somethin' else." She paused and Timony waited while Seymour Steel Cheeks stared at the three new additions to Mae's household with undisguised hostility. "I'm thinkin' it might be useful tomorrow night if Dudley Van Helsing wears his Mae West drag."

"Not a bad idea at that."

"Watch it, Jim. You're agreein' with me about somethin'. It could be catchin'."

For the first time in ages, he smiled. She smiled too and patted his cheek. "Tell Van Helsing where to find us after he gets back from the valley. Tell the other two to follow us in their cars. Give Jake my private phone number. Think of an errand for Seymour. He's poutin' like a small brat, and I don't like lookin' at him when he's like that."

On her way to the door, she stopped to sign autographs, which she did gracefully with an occasional quip that made each athlete think she was a new best friend. In the doorway, she stopped and turned to her worshipers. "I'll be lookin' for you boys on the cards at the arena every Friday night. I'm a steady customer and win or lose, I'll be around to see you in your dressin' rooms. You don't have to worry about lookin' decent. You ain't got nothin' I ain't seen before." While they whooped with laughter, she turned and wiggled her way down the stairs, grasping the handrail for dear life.

SEVEN

THE TAILSPIN CLUB WAS SITUATED ON Sunset Boulevard, a few short blocks below Hollywood Boulevard and across the street from the Palladium Ballroom, where the big swing bands held sway. It was a few yards north of Earl Carroll's theater, where Carroll's seminude Vanities revue was a nightly sellout. Agnes Darwin parked her roadster in the Tailspin's lot and went through the stage door in search of Milton Connery. He was expecting her.

There is nothing so depressing as a nightclub lit by a solitary work light. Two bartenders were at the long bar busy preparing setups for the heavy traffic they were anticipating. A young man sat at an upright piano improvising some riffs. Waiters were setting up tables, and two handymen were diligently waxing the dance floor. There were several workmen perched on stepladders decorating the walls with hobgoblins, skeletons, witches, and black cats under the impatient supervision of one of the club's various managers. This one was Simon LeGrand, a willowy young man with flowing blond locks that reached to his shoulders, which was a fair excuse for the frequent tossing of his head. He wasn't barking orders, he was purring them. He occasionally stamped his foot or looked upward silently seeking succor from a god who had turned his back on him at birth.

The cardboard decorations were beautifully created, and Simon was meticulous about their placement. He held in one hand a diagram of the walls, which he had prepared weeks earlier. Every decoration would be placed where he wanted it placed or he threatened to spit.

Agnes made her way up a short flight of stairs leading to the small stage and the backstage area where dressing rooms and offices were located. She nodded to a stagehand who was assisting another in raising a sequined backdrop up to the flies. She walked straight ahead to a door marked PRIVATE and entered without knocking. Seated behind a desk, Milton Connery said without looking up from a ledger he was studying, "Come right in, Aggie. Make yourself at home: Where'd you park the broomstick?"

"Broomstick gags are getting tiresome." She settled into a chair across from Connery and lit a cigarette. He remained engrossed in the ledger. The sleek son of a bitch, thought Agnes. Jet-black hair, olive skin, strong chin, pencil-lead thin mustache, Bond Street suit and tie. Talk about the immaculate conception.

"How's Mae holding up?" He finally looked up. Handsome bastard, looking several years younger than the fifty she knew him to be.

"Nothing fazes Mae West, not even the threat of death."

The swivel chair groaned for mercy as Connery leaned his large frame back and clasped his hands behind the back of his head. "Shame about Nedda Connolly, she was a good draw."

"Shame about Larry Hopkins and Danny Turallo too. Nice boys. Shame about Neon Light too."

Connery moved forward, hands now lying flat in front of him on top of the desk. "How did he come in to this?"

"Why does it bother you?" She was under attack by a cloud of smoke of her own creation, and she was waving the smoke aside like a semaphore gone berserk.

"Neon's last year's news."

"He's more recent than that. He came into it by way of Mae

West and was introduced by Mae to your old nemesis Herb Villon."

"I didn't know they knew each other."

"As of today they're bosom buddies. Villon and some jerk named Jim Mallory are on the impersonator killings."

"Ain't that just grand?"

"I was at Mae's this morning when they were there hoping to learn something helpful from her."

"Ah, she's not got much to tell them."

"She had them spellbound talking about Neon Light. She told them you were his manager."

"That was no secret."

"It was news to Villon. Villon and Mallory are back digging into Neon's murder."

"How can they do that? It wasn't Villon's case in the first place. It was some schmo who could be played in the movies by Edgar Kennedy."

"Villon is hardly a schmo, as you so quaintly put it. Herbert Villon strikes me as one hell of a smart fellow. From what I heard this morning, I was very impressed by him."

"So what did you hear?" He was lighting a cigarillo, eyes narrowed to protect them from the smoke.

"Villon doesn't think Neon was murdered in Griffith Park. He suspects he was murdered elsewhere and then dumped in the park."

"A logical suspicion."

"Villon thinks Neon was murdered to keep him from spilling some highly select beans."

"What kind of select beans?"

"Orgies. Hidden cameras. Celebrities. Blackmail."

Through a stifled yawn, Connery said, "Oh, that tired old scenario."

"I think Villon suspects it's been freshened up. A neat rewrite that's making it big box office. Does it worry you?"

"I don't like worrying. It leaves lines around the eyes. Remember my eyes? You used to think they were so beautiful until you took to spitting into them."

Agnes favored him with a phony smile. "How nice to know you've been blessed with total recall. How come you booked Mae's sister into the club?"

"What? You gone dumb or something? First of all, she's Mae West's sister and she's a dead ringer for her on top of that. Second of all, she's going to do her Mae West act, and it's topical what with these impersonator murders. Third of all, the publicity we're getting is worth her weight in gold and Friday night's opening is sold out. And tomorrow night's nightmare is almost entirely booked."

"Oh, God! Mae wants a table. A big one. I almost forgot."

"Oi vay, oi vay, oi vay, as my mother used to say when she was sober. How big a table?"

"How big a table you got?" She rattled off what she could remember of Mae's guest list. "Jim Timony, Seymour the Indian gigolo if gigolos are still in style, Herb Villon and girlfriend, Jim Mallory and maybe a girlfriend, and an assortment of bodyguards she's auditioning at Hasseltine's Gym at this very moment."

"Oh, that's good. My customers as you well know favor muscle boys. There'll be lots of squeaks and squeals and trading of phone numbers. I'd better line up the table now." He spoke into his intercom. He instructed a wraith at the other end to arrange for Mae's table. "And where she can be seen by the whole room. Let's make the most of her." He took a puff of the cigarillo, then opened the bottom drawer of his desk and brought forth a fifth of scotch and two glasses. "Could you use a snort?"

"I could use some money."

"That goes without saying, darling, why else are you here?" He set a glass of scotch in front of her and then poured a hearty glassful for himself. "So Mae's bringing the fuzz with her tomorrow night. Knowing her, she's got her sights set on one or both of them."

"She seems genuinely fond of them, but hardly in a motherly way. The vision of Mae West as a mother is as impossible as the vision of Franklin Pangborn as a father." Pangborn was one of the few character actors in films who had made a success with his effeminacy. "Mae told them all she knew about Neon, and it was she who suggested there might be a link between the recent three murders and Neon's."

"Since when did Mae West take to playing detective?"

"Since the cops entered her life."

"Don't she realize she could be playing with fire?"

"If she does, then she'll soon be auditioning firemen." She watched him take a tin box from another drawer, lift the lid, and count out several fifty-dollar bills. "She also put me through some cross-examination."

"About what?"

"About how come I'm connected to you. How come I'm going to be at the party tomorrow night."

"It's a free country. You can go anyplace you like except the men's toilet." He handed Agnes the money, which she swiftly consigned to her handbag. "You tell Mae we were once an item?"

"A very brief item," Agnes stressed as she crossed her legs.

"Aw, come on, Aggie, it wasn't all that bad."

"It wasn't all that good."

"You witch. Villon got any leads?" Connery changed the subject.

"He's got a lot of suspicions. I never can tell a suspicion from a lead, can you?"

"It's pretty obvious to anybody with half a brain that this killer, this vampire if such a thing exists, is practicing for the big time, Miss Mae West in person, in the flesh."

"In the punctured flesh." She was lighting another cigarette while Connery stubbed his cigarillo out in a tray and then poured himself another scotch. Agnes had yet to touch hers. She commented, "Aren't you going a little heavy on the scotch?"

"It's bothering you?"

"Only to the extent I've never seen you drink in broad daylight." She smiled. "Maybe that's because you might be a vampire."

"That ain't funny, Agnes. Like it wasn't very funny when that Edgar Kennedy type questioned me around the clock when Neon was killed."

"How come at the time you never expressed any opinions of your own as to who might have killed Neon? I don't remember hearing any."

"That's because at the time his murder had me talking to myself most of the time. The kid was making great money. I was taking a hefty percentage."

"Milton, did you know he was already dying?"

"Yeah, very tragic."

"Why didn't you tell me?"

"He didn't want anybody to know."

"He told Mae."

"He did?"

"That's what she said."

"I guess he told her, all right. She was everything to him. Mother, father, aunt, uncle, sister, brother, the holy ghost. What other secrets of his was she in on?"

"If there were others, she didn't say. Milton . . ."

"What?"

"Who was Neon Light really?"

Connery said airily, "He wasn't real at all. Like Mae, he was his own creation. He came up from nowhere to somewhere, and that was mostly thanks to Mae West. She taught him everything she knew about drag and female impersonation. You heard of Ray Bourbon?"

"Mae's friend. She mentioned him this afternoon."

"Mae brought him in from the East to work with Neon. Bourbon is one of the all-time great female impersonators. He taught him how to walk, talk, sing. Neon couldn't sing for shit, but by the time Bourbon got through with him, you'd think he was a skylark. I remember how Bourbon compared good female impersonation to good stripping. Gypsy Rose Lee, for instance, the greatest burley-Q stripper in the business today. Ever see her?"

"Once, downtown."

"She ever show any flesh other than her face and her hands?"

"Come to think of it, no."

"That's right. She doesn't show a thing. She strips. She takes things off, but while she's stripping, she talks a blue streak. The chatter's funny, suggestive, an absolute howl. She has the audience paralyzed with laughter and then is off the stage before the suckers realize they ain't seen a thing, not even a flash of a tit. That's what Bourbon taught Neon. How to fake it. Make them think he's singing, when all the time he's talking with the music. But don't get me wrong, Neon was a genuinely gifted mimic. His Mae West was perfection because he was rehearsed by the genuine article. But his Dietrich and his Garbo and all the other ones he did were equally uncanny. Mae was right about one thing. She said Neon could have evolved into a great actor."

"Instead he evolved into a corpse with a crushed skull," Connery said staring into his glass of scotch, a strange expression on his face. Agnes hoped he wasn't going to cry. She couldn't stand the sight of anyone crying, let alone a man. She couldn't remember herself ever having cried. Probably as a child there must have been occasions that called for tears, but as an adult, never. Neon Light. A crushed corpse. Only the skull was crushed, but still, Agnes saw all of the body as crushed. Crushed as a metaphor for disillusion. Could that be it? she wondered. Had a disappointing disillusion added to the killing diseases helped to hasten Neon's departure into a hopefully better afterlife? Neon Light. What a terrible name.

She heard Connery say, "You look like you're smelling rotten eggs."

I'm smelling something rotten, she wanted to say, but instead she said, "I was thinking what a terrible name, Neon Light."

Connery shrugged. "It fit the act. All lit up like a neon light. You saw it yourself. Wasn't he a dazzler?"

"What was his real name?"

"Michael. Michael Williamson."

"Where's his family?"

"He was an orphan."

"Mae said something about a brother."

"Mickey never talked about him, except once when his brother begged him not to do the act. Ah, the hell with it! I don't want to talk about Neon any more. He's dead. Finished. *Kaput.* He's yesterday's news."

"Oh, no he isn't. Villon's digging into his case and Villon is going to find out things somebody wishes he wouldn't."

"What somebody?"

"The somebody who caved in Neon's skull." She finally sipped her scotch. "Mmmm. Nice. Smooth. Like the line you once fed me. So tell me, Milton, got some new dirty pictures I can look at?"

The *Twentieth Century Limited*, the railroad train of the stars, was within twenty-four hours of Los Angeles. It was two days out of Chicago, and the passengers were buzzing with the rumor that Mae West was on board. If she was, she was taking her meals in her drawing room. She had made no appearance as yet in either the club car or the dining car. The porters were unusually circumspect about their mysterious passenger. All they would admit to was, yes, there was a certain Miss West aboard the train. And that certain Miss West kept herself busy manicuring her nails, trying on an assortment of Mae West dresses that were in surprisingly excellent condition, singing to herself in her husky, sexy voice, and spending an hour or two reading selections from the stack of magazines she'd brought on board with her. These included *True Romances*, *Liberty*, *Photoplay*, *Screenland*, *Picture Play*, and *Strength and Health*, where she oohed and aaahed over the illustrations of muscular athletes.

Now forty-eight hours of self-imposed isolation were beginning to wear on Beverly West's nerves. It was also her frustration that her only masculine contacts were with colored porters, whom she tipped handsomely not to reveal that she was the secondary West on the train. "The hell with this," she said to herself, "I gotta spring myself out of solitary or I'll go bananas." She selected a Hattie Carnegie creation that was daringly décolleté. She gilded her fingers from her large assortment of paste diamond rings. She artfully positioned several feathers in her platinum-blond hair. She draped a feather boa around her shoulders, selected a fan that she maneuvered professionally, and then left the drawing room where a porter waited to guide her to the dining car. It was a journey not without its hazards. She stopped to give autographs. She graciously posed for snapshots. She peppered the air with quips and comments, and her dazzled audience was unaware that unlike her clever sister, Beverly's quips and comments were secondhand, cribbed not only from Mae's repertoire but from some ancient joke books given to her by an alcoholic comedian.

Arriving in the club car, there were more requests for autographs, and the club car pianist, who made the trip once a week for a barely livable stipend, dutifully played "Frankie and Johnny." She mouthed "Thank you" to the pianist, who couldn't wait to get back to Chicago to tell his friends that Mae West looked like an ambulatory matzo ball. Beverly settled into an easy chair and told an eager waiter she'd like a very dry sherry. A small table separated her from a fellow traveler, a middle-age gentleman who, before lighting a meerschaum pipe, asked Beverly if its smell might offend her.

"Why, heavens no," said Beverly in her excellent Mae West drawl, "just so long you don't grind your teeth on the stem. It's the grindin' of teeth I can't tolerate. Especially when it's someone sleepin' next to me what's grindin' 'em."

"You *are* Miss West, aren't you?"

Thank God he hadn't asked if she was *Mae* West. Mae had warned her often if she ever claimed to be the star, she'd have her put behind bars. Beverly smiled and drawled, "Why yes, big boy, how'd yuh recognize me under my travelin' disguise?"

"Miss West, there ain't no way you could disguise yourself."

"Sure there is," said Beverly with shameless self-assurance, "I could put on blackface and claim I'm Louise Beavers." Louise Beavers was a fine colored actress who had scored two years before in the screen version of the Fannie Hurst novel, *Imitation of Life.*

72

The waiter brought the dry sherry. "I think you'll find this dry enough."

"I hope I do," said Beverly. "I can't stand wet sherry just like I can't stand wet men." She tasted it. "Very nice." The waiter smiled and left. "Big boy, you got me at a disadvantage. You know who I am. Now I don't know who you are. I mean, yuh look a lot like my friend Victor McLaglen, but I know you ain't him because he's in Hollywood doin' a movie with that kid Freddie Bartholomew. Whaddya say, big boy, do I get to hear yuh monicker?"

"My name is Max Collins."

"Max Collins. Any relation to Tom Collins?"

"I don't know any Tom Collins."

"Tom Collins is a drink." He looked blank. "Don't strain yourself."

"Are you traveling alone, Miss West?"

"Why, come to think of it, I am. I think it was Albert Einstein what said, 'You travel faster when you travel alone,' or somethin' smart like that." She took another dainty sip, restraining successfully the urge to down it in one gulp. "Are you travelin' alone too?"

"I'm most delightedly am. Is Los Angeles your destination?"

"That's where the train's headin', ain't it?" She thought, I think I've landed me a dummy. He ain't bad-lookin' and he's built good, but don't he know the *Twentieth Century* only goes to Los Angeles?

"May I offer you another sherry?" he asked gently.

"Well, I ain't quite finished this one, but I guess by the time another one gets here, I'll be ready for it." Max signaled the waiter for a new round of drinks. He was having a Manhattan cocktail and thoughtfully offered Beverly the cherry.

"No thanks, Max. I ain't big on cherries."

"Miss West, do I dare? Would you do me the honor? I mean, since we're both traveling alone, would you have dinner with me?"

"Well, Max, I was thinkin' of dinin' in the privacy of my

drawin' room, like I been doin' the past two nights. It ain't much fun, but, y'see, I don't like people starin' at me when I'm eatin'. I don't suppose you been dinin' in the privacy of your drawin' room?''

"I don't have one. I have a lower berth."

"But I'm sure you're from an upper class. You're starin' at me. Somethin' wrong?''

"Honestly, I'm thinking you're either very brave or very foolish."

"Why's that?"

"Don't you feel the danger of traveling unaccompanied while there's some killer out there murdering your impersonators?''

"Why, big boy, he's in Los Angeles. He ain't on this train."

"How can you be sure?"

"Well, I had a hard time gettin' myself on. Paramount Pitchers got somebody bumped so I could get my drawin' room. So how could the killer get on?'' She laughed. "Nobody except Paramount knows I'm on this train. Hey, now wait a minute, big boy? You ain't suggestin' you could be the killer?''

"Me? A killer?'' He laughed as the waiter served the fresh drinks. Max handed him a dollar tip. A dollar tip in those depression days was abnormally generous. The waiter thanked him with the profusion of a child seeking adoption. As the man backed away obsequiously, Beverly opened the fan and waved it back and forth under her face.

"What a lovely fan,'' commented Max. "Is it Spanish?''

"It's an airloom. It was handed down from a lot of degenerations. It's Eye-talian.''

"It is rather warm in here, come to think of it."

"I got a fan in my room. An electric one, that is. I think it'd be fun to have dinner with you, Max, if don't mind goin' halfies on my solitude.''

"I'd be honored to go halfies, as you so quaintly put it, on your anything.''

"Let's go when we finish our drinks. By the way, Max, what's your profession?"

"I'm a professional masseur."

Beverly's eyes widened with delight. "Well, here's hopin' you don't rub me the wrong way."

EIGHT

In the limousine returning from Hasselstine's Gym, Mae wondered aloud, "I didn't want to ask Jake what's with that black patch over his right eye. I didn't want to hurt his feelings any in case that patch was covering a bad injury. You know anything about it, Jim?"

"He's had a cataract removed."

"Oh, so then he'll be able to see again as good as new. You know, you're missin' some of the best parts if you can only see me with one eye. Well, whaddya think of my bodyguards?"

"Physically they're superb examples of young American manhood."

"Stop talkin' like a politician up for reelection. You've gotten very pompous out here, Jim. What's become of the Good Time Charlie you used to be? The hearty laugh, the slap on the back, the dumb jokes, the bimbos on each arm when you went to Texas Guinan's club? Out here, Jim, you're like a spayed cat. Still full of good intentions but no way how to use them."

"You spayed the cat, Mae. I get older. You don't age at all."

"That's because I think young. I'm keepin' up with the times. That's why I'm always battlin' them sunnuva bitches at Paramount. I can go ten rounds with them anytime I like before I score the knockout. I ain't no second-class citizen like the rest of the ladies they've got under contract except for maybe that Miriam Hopkins dame who screams a lot. It ain't enough for me that I've got the vote, I've also got to let them know I've got the clout. Years from now the world will look back on me, especially women, and they'll thank me for bein' one of the first to liberate us girls. Me and my good friend Eleanor Roosevelt. I wonder if she's ever gonna take my suggestions about gettin' her teeth fixed. But I'm digressin', and y'know I don't like strayin' from the straight and narrow." She smiled a sly smile as she examined the fingernails of her right hand. "Although every now and then I manage to stray . . . and stray . . . and stray . . . Seymour!" she shouted. "Stop drivin' so reckless. Y'know I'm a nervous passenger."

"I'm only doing forty, for crying out loud!"

"Well, in this cemetery that's reckless drivin'." She returned her attention to Timony. "Jim, we can't keep beatin' around the bush. The leaves are fallin' off and the branches are lookin' sick and skinny."

"Save your breath, Mae."

"I will if it'll draw any interest."

"You'll always draw interest, Mae. You're the eighth wonder of the world."

"Oh, yeah? Who's the other seven ahead of me?"

He reached over and gently held her hand. She refrained from jerking it away as she had been doing of late when he tried to make the gesture. She could tell from his soft tone of voice, the bittersweet expression on his face, that he knew their business relationship had reached the end of the line, that all that remained ahead were impassable lines. "You don't need me anymore, Mae. And I'm not very happy out here. The oranges and the lemons are getting on my nerves. Making movies isn't for me. I need a nickel player piano in a saloon with sawdust on the floor and some pool tables and slot machines in the back room. I need a poker game with jacks or better to open and a slug of bourbon with a beer chaser at my table. But more than that, I need a soft, feminine shoulder to lay my head on, and there's no longer a receptive one in my immediate vicinity. I know you understand and you sympathize, and now you don't have to talk to me through clenched teeth any longer."

"I'm sorry for that, Jim. You know I got a few good virtues, but patience ain't one of them. How soon are you plannin' to leave?"

"I thought I'd better stick around until the killer is caught. If I left now, it would look as though I was running out on you in your time of need or else I'm the guilty party and taking it on the lam."

Mae chuckled. "I'm sure many's a time you've thought of provin' I'm not immortal."

"Oh, yes indeed, Miss West. Many, many a time."

"When you're ready, we'll settle up. Now don't say a word. For years you were as much Mae West as I am except my curves are better. I know you've got plenty salted away but I'll sleep better knowin' you've got more, like maybe a nice annuity that'll give you a comfortable yearly income."

Seymour's ears were burning. A nice annuity. A comfortable yearly income. Me too, please God, me too.

"Now, gettin' back to the muscle boys. I think they should be packin' rods. Get in touch with a dealer, Jim, and let's buy the boys shooters they can handle. Maybe we can get Villon and Mallory to have them over to the precinct a couple of hours tomorrow morning and give them a pernter or two. And another thing. My apartment house. We ain't got no doorman. In fact, there are two things that are rare in this town, kind hearts and doormen. I want you to hire a doorman. I think a retired cop would make sense, but not too retired. Villon ought to be able to help us there. In fact, try to get three of them so we've got front-door protection around the clock, eight hours each. And I don't want them hired temporary, I want these guys to know they got permanent positions, financial security, because my reputation for generosity is right on the nose."

Seymour asked anxiously, "What about me? What do I do?"

"What you're doin' now, Seymour, you're doin' just fine,

and I don't mean drivin' this crate. We're home. And I'm hungry."

Entering the apartment after kissing the mezuzah (and sternly instructing Timony and Seymour to do likewise), Mae sauntered into the kitchen where Goneril was preparing a chicken for roasting and Desdemona sat on a stool at a counter shelling peas. "Ladies, I'm hungry."

Goneril warned her good-naturedly, "This chicken will take at least two hours before it's roasted properly."

"Yeah, that's always the way with chicken. Desdemona . . ."

"Yes, ma'am?"

"Peel me a kumquat." She took off the picture hat, kicked off her shoes, and sat on a chair. "Now, ladies, I want to prepare you for some changes that are being made around here as of right now."

The sisters exchanged looks and Goneril asked with anxiety, "Ain't you happy with us no more?"

Mae was startled. "Sure I am. What makes you think I'm dissatisfied? Why, if I was a lesbeen your lives would be in danger. Fortunately God saw to it that I ain't. What's the matter with you dummies? Have you forgotten there's a madman out there possibly lookin' to cook my goose, and he don't need no *Fanny Farmer Cookbook* to tell him how. I've hired myself some protection. Three big boys over six feet tall each of them, and with muscles as big as billboards advertising Mae West's available. There's one gorgeous black brute—"

"Hallelujah!" cried Desdemona.

"Amen!" seconded Goneril.

"Why, you wicked creatures you," said Mae as she watched Desdemona peel the kumquat with trembling hands. "He's been hired to protect me, not himself. But from the look of him, there's enough for everyone. Those knees of his look as though he could crush watermelons without spilling a drop. Anyway, let's get back to bein' serious. There's that empty apartment next to yours. Desdemona, ain't you finished laceratin' that piece of fruit? Goneril, I want you to track down someplace that rents furniture. We'll need three single beds, some dressers and bureaus where they can store their belongin's, a refrigerator, a table and chairs, a radio, a sofa, some easy chairs, enough lamps for them to see by let alone read by although one of them, a tall redhead with a lot of freckles, looks like the readin' type, and plenty of towels and linens. Then see they've got plenty of soap, stuff like that. Goneril, I assured them you'll be doin' their meals so for the extra work, I'm promisin' you a nice bonus."

"You don't have to do that, Miss West. If they's here to protect you then I'm more then proud to do for them." Goneril roared with laughter. "And I promise you I'll be doin' my best."

"I'm sure you will. My money's on your nose. Now, as to your main target, Selma Jefferson Burr—"

"Selma?!" they exclaimed together. Mae explained the origin of his first name.

"Don't that beat all," said Desdemona, placing the peeled kumquat on a plate and serving it to Mae with a fruit knife. Mae ignored the knife and took a merciless bite out of the delicate fruit.

While chewing, Mae continued with her current favorite subject. She named the other two men and then advised them Timony was hiring three doormen for round-the-clock protection.

"That's the best idea yet," said Goneril. "Most nights when I'm walking home alone I walk real fast because I'm afraid some thug will jump out from behind all the damned hedges on this street and attack and rape me."

"Well, it hasn't happened yet," said Mae.

"Dammit no," said Goneril, and shrieked with laughter.

"Girls," said Mae as the laughter finally subsided, "you are my treasures. What would I do without you? Desdemona, anybody phone?"

"Miss Darwin the witch. She said to tell you you've got a big table for tomorrow night."

"I hope it's big enough. I'll work on the seating arrangements and the place cards tonight. I want to do it right, according to Herle, like the Countess de Frasso taught me. Christ . . ." She struck her forehead lightly with the palm of her hand. "I almost forgot my sister gets in tomorrow. Desdemona, have you got the guest room prepared?"

"Oh, yes ma'am, lots of bath salts in the bathroom, plenty of scented soap, lots of heavy drapes in the bedroom to keep the sun out in the morning so she can sleep late, and I hope you don't mind but I hung some of them dirty etchin's of yours."

"If you're talkin' about them Tintoretto prints, they ain't dirty, they're artistic."

"It's a good thing our mammy won't see them or she'd be washin' all our mouths out with laundry soap."

Goneril snorted. "Come off it, Desdemona. Mammy wouldn't mind one bit, what with all them uncles she used to bring home to spend the night with her." They were shrieking with laughter again.

"Uncles, eh?" said Mae, laughing with them and feeling delightfully buoyant despite the danger lurking outside, albeit unseen, no less threatening.

"Okay, girls, settle down. Now you ain't met Beverly, so let me give you a couple of tips on how to deal with her. First of all, she looks just like me. She walks like me, she talks like me, and she spends money like me because I'm very generous with her allowance. She drinks dry sherry so, Goneril, order a case and make sure it's good stuff. She dresses like me because she's wearin' my cast-off things. Now, you know me well enough to know I ain't got no cheap side, it's just that it gives Bev a good feelin' to be wearin' what I used to wear. There's one serious problem that could crop up and you'll have to deal with it any way you see fit. If it gets real troublesome, then tell me about it and I'll deal with it personally." She cleared her throat. "Every so often Beverly gets the delusion that *she's* Mae West. She used to do it in public a lot until I found out about it and threatened to step on her neck, that is, if I could find it. When she thinks she's me, she gets very loud and bossy."

"Why, Miss West you ain't never bossy," said Desdemona.

"I know I ain't but I'm just warnin' you about Beverly. Hey, wait a minute. You tellin' me I'm loud?" she shouted, and the women were off on another laughing binge. Mae stared at them, smiling, hands on hips, and then said, "Okay, girls, settle down. Now, Beverly opens at the Tailspin Club Friday night."

"Oh, yes?" said Goneril. "What she doin', singin'?"

"What do you expect her to be doin' when she looks like me, walks like me, talks like me, and there, from what I've heard from a few gents we once had in common, the resemblance ends. She's impersonatin' me."

"Ain't we got enough of those?" asked Goneril.

"As far as the real thing's concerned, the answer is yes. But according to this murderer, he's probably worried he's runnin' out of material. So along comes Beverly to maybe stoke his furnace. Well, we'll cope. I gotta make a phone call. Goneril, ain't you got that chicken in the oven yet?"

"Right away, Miss West. Right away!"

Mae left the kitchen, sauntered across the living room where Timony and Seymour were seated at a card table engrossed in a game of casino. She entered her sumptuous bedroom, undressed slowly while humming an assortment of show tunes. She slipped into a diaphanous negligee and then sat on her white swan bed, which was shaped like a Venetian gondola, but definitely wide enough to accommodate a companion. She reached for her white telephone and then cursed under her breath. Villon's number was in her handbag, and she'd left that and her picture hat in the kitchen. On cue, there was a tap at her door. Mae yelled "Entah!" and Desdemona entered carrying picture hat and handbag. She placed the hat on a table and gave the handbag to Mae. "Honey, this is mental telepathy." Mae found Villon's number and dialed.

Herb Villon was alone in his office, studying his accumulation of notes about the imposter murders. The phone rang and he said, "Villon."

"Hello there, tall, dark, and swarthy," purred Mae.

Villon smiled. She had her Mae West act perfected to a T. He could picture her sitting with one hand on her hip. He wondered if she slept with one hand on her hip. "How you holding up, Mae?"

"Whaddya mean, how'm I holdin' up? You make it sound like I could use some props under me."

Villon hastily reassured her, "That's not how I meant it."

"I know, I know. I was only pullin' your leg." She was wondering what it would be like to pull his leg; he was wondering what it would be like to have her pulling his leg. He was feeling strangely warm. "Now listen, Herb, before we settle down into idle chatter, let me tell you about how I've been surroundin' myself with security." She told him the names of the three she'd hired as bodyguards and he jotted them down on his pad. "Two of the boys followed us home in their cars and I got them sittin' in the foyer downstairs while I wait for one of my girls to line up the furniture for the apartment they'll occupy on the floor under mine. As a matter of fact, they're probably wonderin' if I've abandoned them. Hold the line a minute." She sauntered to the door, opened it, and sent Seymour to fetch Salvatore Puccini and Selma Jefferson Burr. "And, Seymour, put a note on the outside door for Dudley Van Helsing to ring the top floor when he gets here. I hope that ain't too heavy a load for you." Without waiting for any response, she shut the door and returned to the bed and the phone.

"You still there, Herb?"

"Riveted to my chair."

She told him about wanting to hire some ex-policemen as doormen. "You got any layin' around in your vicinity?"

"I'll put Jim Mallory on it right away. There's bound to be some retirees bored with retirement and anxious to get away from their wives and back to the outside world."

"I'm sure it'll rejuvenate them if you tell them they'll be workin' for Mae West. Now about tomorrow night. You ain't forgot we're goin' to the party at the Tailspin Club."

"Of course not."

"Who you bringin'?"

"A friend of mine. Her name's Hazel Dickson."

"Hazel Dickson. That rings a bell." She snapped her fingers. "She's a writer."

"If you want to call it that."

"She's tried to get me for an interview. Well, she's okay with me as long as she doesn't try spendin' the night buggin' me. We'll also have my sister Beverly with us. She gets in tomorrow on the *Twentieth Century Limited*. The train may be limited, but Beverly ain't. Agnes the witch'll be there of course, but I think she'll be spendin' the evenin' floatin' around. Of course there'll be Milton Connery, and I'll try to behave like a lady when he's around. I can't stand the bastard. It's not a very polite term but back in Brooklyn we'd call him a greaseball."

"We use the term here too." She couldn't see it, but he was smiling. "But only in private. There are so many actors out here to whom the nasty word applies."

"What about Jim Mallory? Who's he bringin'?"

"No one, as far as I know."

"Well then, that's just fine. He can be Beverly's date. She's a little old for him, but she's good for a couple of laughs. Just warn him not to confuse us, we're that alike thanks to the years she's been practicin'." She shook her head from side to side while thinking of Beverly and the coming weeks together. "Now listen, Herb, Jim Timony thinks I should ask you to check up on my bodyguards just in case one or all of them has a record. It won't make no difference to me either way because I'm no Indian giver. Once I hire them, they stay hired, unless they get a better offer and then I let them go unless we're in the middle of somethin'." She smiled. "If you get my drift. Now, Herb, do you mind if I get serious for a minute or two?"

"Not at all. What's on your mind?"

"The witch. Agnes. We discussed her earlier today, but I been doin' some heavy thinkin' since then. I told you she and Milton Connery were once an item, but you know, I think she's still mixed up with him. I don't mean romantically anymore, I mean I suspect she knows what's goin' on behind the scenes there. Am I soundin' disloyal? We're good friends, but still, as my mother used to say when she thought my father was strayin' off the path, you can't turn a blind eye to any hanky panky, especially if you suspect there's more panky than hanky. You still there?"

"Sure. Would I leave you in midsentence?"

"Maybe you would, dependin' on the sentence. Anyway, she lives real swell. You know what I mean. She's got this nice bungalow on DeLongpre, not the greatest neighborhood in the world, but come to think of it, neither is mine. The place is beautifully furnished and she's got some real genyoowine antiques. You know, old stuff with worm holes in them. It's not to my taste, but then, I'm very particular about what I find tasteful. She spends a lot of money on clothes and shoes, and I know because I've poked around in her closets. Now, I don't know how much money you're supposed to earn from witchin' around, but it seems to me she spends more time hangin' around with me than she does hangin' around with a steady job. Not even a part-time job."

"I thought she got hired for private parties. I assume she's been hired tomorrow night to be a guest witch."

"Yeah, that makes sense. I know she gets paid to tell fortunes and reads those spooky cards—"

"Tarot cards."

"That's it. She tried readin' me once but I don't have to be told my future and I sure don't need to be reminded of my past. Especially in this hot climate, mmmmmm." She liked the way he laughed. It was smooth like the motor in a Rolls-Royce. His laugh had class. Quiet, sincere, dependable. "And another thing. She's never tried to put the bite on me like too many deadbeats I can tell you about. Now, she was still bein' romanced by Connery when he was managin' Neon Light. Even so, she insists she knows very little about Neon. Not his real name, not about his background, nothin'."

"Well, apparently you got more out of him than anyone else. Possibly Milton Connery knows things he's not about to reveal to anyone."

"You could pull him in and rubber hose him."

"Mae West, for shame. Are you insinuating the police use rubber hoses to beat suspects?"

"I ain't insinuatin', honey, I'm tellin' you. I been around cops all my life. I know what goes on in them soundproof basement rooms. I been in a couple of them."

"Beaten with a rubber hose?"

"Mr. Detective, I've done soundproof rooms for better reasons, mmmmmmmm. Anyway, before I tear myself away from the phone, you got any leads, any fresh clues?"

"Jim's tracked down Neon's file. It's in cold storage in the basement."

"That don't sound too good. Can't you dig it out?"

"It's being dug out. If I have to go down there and do the digging myself."

"He ain't been dead all that long. Shouldn't somebody still be workin' on his case?"

"There should." He bristled quietly. "I'm going to talk to the detective who was assigned to it. I haven't seen him around today."

Mae was angry at the thought of Neon's case being shunted aside like an old shoe. "Now you give him a piece of your mind, but not too good a piece. I mean, I'm positive Neon connects to the three vampire victims."

"He does, besides the fact they had their profession in common, they all worked the Tailspin Club, and they all knew Milton Connery."

"Let me tell you something, Herb, he's perfect casting for a vampire."

"Ah, Mae, if only it was all that easy."

"Meanin' what?"

"Meaning pinning this on Connery because you think he looks like a vampire."

"I ain't pinnin' this on anybody. That job is up to you, and I know you and me got one important thing in common."

"What's that?"

"Like them Canadian cops on horseback, we always get our man."

Five minutes later Mae, having changed into a less revealing housecoat, entered the living room to find Desdemona plying Selma and Salvatore with cheese and crackers. "Well, I'm glad to see you're gettin' along so well. Is Goneril in the kitchen?"

"No, I'm right here," said Goneril, entering with a tray that held a plate of chopped chicken livers, some sliced bologna, and a basket of sliced rye bread and pumpernickel.

Mae surveyed the tray and asked wryly, "No caviar?"

"We's fresh out. I just phoned the delicatessen to order some."

Desdemona was saying to Selma Jefferson Burr, "Now, honey, you help yourself to that chopped liver. It's made with fresh chicken fat and chopped onions." She said to Salvatore Puccini, "You looks a little pale honey, you better dig in."

Mae noticed Timony and Seymour had abandoned the card table, leaving the deck of cards neatly stacked. Mae asked Desdemona where they'd gone to.

"Oh, they's gone to buy some gats," she said airily, as though the purchase of handguns was a common occurrence in the household.

"Goneril, what about the furniture for the boys?"

"Well, let me tell you—"

"I'm listenin' and it better have a happy endin'."

"Well, first they tells me it will take at least three days for delivery—"

"What's their number? Let *me* talk to them." Mae was always spoiling for a fight.

"Now just a minute, Miss Mae, I been with you long enough to know we don't give up that easy. Then they says they need a deposit and a month's rent in advance. So I says, you'll get those when you deliver them today and I don't mean eight o'clock or nine o'clock or two minutes past midnight. You are talking to a lady what works for the one and the only and the celebrated movie star, Miss Mae West." She paused. "Of course they didn't believe me."

Mae had her hands on the hips again, which meant she'd see

that furniture delivered within an hour or else. "Give me that number."

"Now be patient, Miss Mae. I says, I didn't expect you to so I says, Hold the phone, Miss West will speak to you herself."

Mae said to the ceiling, "I don't believe this."

Goneril had her impersonation down pat, and Mae was astonished and then laughing. "So when I finishes, they says they wants autographed pictures, and I says, 'Sure, boys, I'd sign 'em in blood but I'm a little anemic this week, mmmmm.' "

Mae said, "Goneril, you and Desdemona will never cease to amaze me. When are they deliverin' the stuff?"

"The place is on Fairfax. That's ten minutes from here. Dependin' on how fast they can load the truck, they should be here in an hour or so."

The door chimed. Desdemona hurried to it and gasped at Dudley Van Helsing's bright red hair and freckled face.

"Come on in, Dudley. Meet Desdemona and Goneril. Put your stuff there until you move downstairs. Help yourself to some nosh."

"Miss West," Dudley said gravely, "I don't think it's a wise idea to leave the downstairs door unattended."

"You're right, Dudley, and I'm hirin' three doormen for eight-hour shifts. But you have to understand, before a murderer was on the loose, everybody in these parts left their doors unlocked. I can't have ours locked because I don't have keys for the other tenants. So we'll have to look to the good Lord for protection until Herb Villon—that's the detective in charge of the case—finds me some retired flatfeet to take over at the door. Meantime, boys, the furniture for your apartment should be arrivin' within the hour and while we're waitin', I'll tell you about what you'll be doin' tomorrow. Selma, don't bolt your food like that, it's bad for your digestion."

Delilah wagged a finger back and forth at Selma. He grinned the fabulous grin, and Delilah's heartbeat accelerated.

"I want you boys to get a real good night's sleep because I've got an early call at Paramount Pitchers tomorrow mornin'. I'm shootin' a new movie and today's been my first day off, there won't be any more I don't think. So you'll be with me at the studio all day."

Their faces brightened at the promise of what a day at a Hollywood studio might offer. Puccini asked shyly, "Er, Miss West, do you suppose I could meet Carole Lombard?"

"If she's on the lot, it's possible. She's a good Joe and very democratic. Now I'm warnin' you, makin' movies is very boring. But while keepin' an eye on me you can also keep in trainin'. You know, like sparrin' around and shadow boxin'. Then tomorrow night, tomorrow you know bein' Hallowe'en, we're goin' to a party at the Tailspin Club. Herb Villon will be there with this girlfriend and his fellow detective Jim Mallory. Then you've got my sister Beverly to contend with. She's arrivin' in town tomorrow and I'm warnin' you, she's a maneater and you three are just the kind of smorgasbord she goes for. What's the matter, Dudley? What's eatin' you?"

"I can contend with a maneater. But the Tailspin on Hallowe'en night. I have an idea we three are going to need a little protection of our own."

Mae grinned. "I don't need no witch to tell me tomorrow night feels like it's gonna be a very interestin' night!"

NINE

THE DETECTIVE STANDING IN THE DOORWAY of Herb Villon's office was named Felix Dvorack. Villon described him as being slightly better looking then a Boston bull. He had a beer belly and wore a stained vest under his stained jacket. He chewed on a cigar stub and kept his thumbs jammed behind the waistline of his stained trousers. There was always stubble on his chin. Villon made it a point to avoid a face-to-face confrontation with him as it meant the possibility of asphyxiation by the garlic fumes reeking from his mouth. They loathed each other. Dvorack referred to Villon as the Big Shot, occasionally he'd nastily refer to him as Fancy Pants, and was jealous of his acquaintance with several celebrities. Villon was admired and respected by his peers and his superiors. Dvorack was tolerated though Mallory referred to him as the Bubonic Plague and wished science would stamp him out.

Villon stared at Dvorack with disguised distaste. "You going to stand in the doorway or are you coming in?"

Dvorack didn't move. "The desk told me you wanted to see me the minute I got back. Well, I'm back more than a minute. That bother you?"

Someday, thought Villon, I'm going to smack you in the mouth and send that filthy cigar stub all the way down into

90

your bowels. "Felix, what bothers me is your sudden paralysis. Can you come into the room and sit down, or shall I come out into the hall where"—he couldn't resist the dig—"the air is considerably fresher."

Dvorack stared at Villon who resumed working on his notes, knowing Dvorack would soon be sitting opposite him. The man had no guts. He couldn't outface anyone. He knew he was disliked. He was lonely. He was a bachelor. Villon suspected he would never live to a mythical ripe old age. Herb heard the door shut. Dvorack walked heavily the few feet to a chair on the opposite side of the desk. He settled his overweight bulk into the chair as Villon looked up. The cigar stub was an obscenity. There was always a stub, just as it seemed there was always Felix Dvorack. The only compensation was that Dvorack's retirement was promised before the end of the year.

"Well, Villon?" Dvorack pronounced it Villain, deliberately.

"Neon Light."

Dvorack obviously didn't like hearing the name again. Villon could see it in his face.

"Well, Felix?" Villon didn't try to mask his impatience.

"Well, what?"

"Why'd you put his file on ice?"

"Because it was finished."

"You nabbed his killer?"

"Don't be funny. You ain't no Jack Benny."

"You're no detective."

Dvorack moved forward, his fists clenched. "You looking for trouble?"

"No, Felix, you've been looking for trouble and you've found it. I had a long talk with the chief about Neon Light's case and the file being buried in the basement, and he told me to have it out with you because if he did, and you know his temper, you'd be back pounding a beat. He doesn't want to do it to you with you so close to retirement." He pointed a finger at Dvorack, who recognized when Villon meant business and could feel his armpits dampening. "Who told you to sink that file?"

"Nobody told me nothing. I did it all by myself."

Villon's voice rose an octave. "You've got no authority to close a case without first talking to the chief and the rest of us! Where the hell do you get off pulling that file?"

"I came to a fucking dead end. There was noplace else to go, so I sank it. So what? Some faggot gets his skull bashed in in Griffith Park. Big deal! They're always getting killed there. Who gives a shit about a fucking fairy?"

Villon was on his feet, his hands on the desk, his face a frightening mask of snarling fury. "A good cop gives a shit! Did you get paid to bury that file?"

Dvorack's face was ashen. "You son of a bitch . . ." His voice was low and menacing.

Villon spit each word. "Did you get paid to bury that file? Don't horse around with me, Felix. I've long suspected you had your hand in Milton Connery's pocket!"

"Bastard. I hate your guts."

"You'd be a bigger asshole than you are if you didn't. As of now we don't have to make believe and be polite to each other. Like every cop in this precinct, I can't wait to see you walking out of the front door forever. You stink, Felix, not just your clothes and your filthy cigar butts and your body, you just plain stink as a person. Neon Light was a person. A brilliant talent who was admired and respected, and he's not to be swept under a carpet or buried in the fucking basement. I'm melting that ice right now, Felix, that file is being dug up, not only because his case has been reassigned to me—"

"You son of a bitch!"

"—but because it's tied in with the vampire killings."

"Balls!"

"If you weren't so quick to bury it, you'd realize Neon also did a Mae West impersonation. He had the honor to open the show. The first of the vampire's victims."

"He wasn't. It's a coinci—" Dvorack stopped abruptly. His

eyes were blinking nervously. Villon's eyes were riveted to Dvorack's face.

"It's a coincidence? How do you know?"

"I don't know for sure. I mean . . . I mean . . . even though I sank the file, and you're right . . . you're right, Herb, you're absolutely right." He was in the hot seat and squirming. "Like I said, even though I sank the file, I been thinking . . . y'know, it comes slow to me, I been thinking—Gee, Neon was also an impersonator, maybe I was too quick, maybe there's a connection with him and these vampire killings . . ."

"Then why didn't you bring his file up?"

"I—I didn't want to be too hasty, I wanted to be sure, y'know?"

"I know. I know you've had four months to recover the file. Four months in which three more impersonators were killed, and one was a woman, positively no faggot, Felix, positively no faggot." He sat down. He was trembling. "When'd you bury the file?" Dvorack licked his lips. "You buried it before these last three murders. You buried it maybe a few weeks after Neon Light was buried. Real quick investigation, Felix. Real fast to decide you'd reached a fucking dead end. Oh, boy, am I looking forward to reading that file. I'll bet I find you did next to nothing to try and get a lead on Neon's murderer. I'll bet there isn't a mention of Milton Connery in it."

Dvorack blustered, "Come off it! Connery was his manager. He was very cooperative."

"I'll bet he was. Why didn't you talk to Mae West?"

"Mae West? That whore!" Villon almost leapt across the desk to strangle Dvorack, but he was quick to realize if he did, he'd be subjected to a disciplinary embarrassment for attacking a brother officer. Some brother.

From the way Villon stared, Dvorack realized "whore" was a mistake. He knew Villon was assigned the vampire case, a case he had campaigned to get for himself and had been flatly rejected, his chief struggling to keep from laughing in his face.

Villon felt his temples throbbing. He stared into the other man's face with undisguised revulsion and loathing. He finally spoke after what Dvorack found to be a long and uncomfortable silence. "Mae West is the kind of wonderful human being you can never hope to be. Mae West was Neon Light's friend. She encouraged him. She helped create his act. Without her telling me, I know she supported him financially until he made it on his own. And to show you what a fine detective that lady is, and I mean lady in the royal sense, that lady pointed out to me that Neon Light is very likely connected to the vampire killings because he also impersonated Miss West." He leaned forward. "And let me tell you this, Felix, if I find out you've been on the take, if I find out you're a rogue cop, I will personally bring you up on charges and see to it that they stick and then you can take your retirement and shove it where it belongs because you'll be out on your ass a disgrace."

Jim Mallory had quietly come into the office and stood against the door. Dvorack was unaware of his presence. Jim had heard most of Villon's peroration. He had never heard such vituperation coming from this man whom he loved and admired, with whom he had worked so happily these many years. It was a revelation and he loved it. It was a side of Villon he'd longed to see. Calm, cool, collected Herb Villon, keeping all that anger locked inside. Mallory suspected he must have an ulcer the size of a golf ball.

"Who paid you?" Villon wasn't letting the fish off the hook. "I'll make you a promise. It's between you and me and Mallory."

"Mallory? Why Mallory?"

"Because he's standing behind you and he's famous for his excellent hearing."

Dvorack didn't bother looking for Mallory. His eyes were glued to Villon.

Villon said, "I won't breathe a word of it to the chief until you're out of here forever. Now repeat after me: Milton Connery."

Dvorack finally removed the cigar butt from his mouth and put it into an ashtray on the desk. "He's done me lots of favors, Herb. Lots of favors. I owe him. I know it's wrong, it's very wrong. But I saw no way to break Neon Light's case. There were no clues. No leads."

"There could have been plenty of clues, plenty of leads if you'd conducted an honest investigation. If you'd interviewed Miss West, the other impersonators Neon knew and was friendly with, the staff at the Tailspin Club. If you'd dug into Neon's past and found where he came from."

"I did that! I did that! He was an orphan. He was adopted by this couple named Williamson."

"Did you talk to them?"

"Yeah, yeah, sure I did. They told me he had an older brother but they didn't know who he was or where he was."

"So why did you stop there?"

"I didn't stop there. Who told you I stopped there? I kept digging. I *did* talk to the staff at the Tailspin. I even got tipped to talk to that witch, Agnes something."

"Agnes Darwin, Connery's watering hole at the time."

"Oh. So that was it. I didn't get much from her. Nothing that was of use." He said heatedly, "I was getting close. I was getting real close. I found out about the after-hours orgies with all them Hollywood big shots and the hidden cameras and the blackmail."

"Is that in the file?" Villon asked quickly.

"Huh?"

"You heard me. I talk plain and clear."

"It's not in the file."

"Why not?"

"I—I—I didn't think it had anything to do with Neon's murder."

"Supposing I tell you it's going to have everything to do with Neon's murder." Dvorack seemed to have gotten smaller. Although he couldn't see his face, Mallory imagined that the Boston bull now looked like an obscene baby. His shoulders had sagged and Mallory imagined he'd grow smaller and smaller and then something would come along to mercifully blow him away into oblivion.

Villon shifted in his seat. He couldn't believe it, but he was feeling sorry for the man. He'd had no idea his meeting with Dvorack would lead to the man's destruction and physical disintegration. He only wanted to know why he had hidden the file. It was fascinating to be a detective. And to think that as a teenager he'd spent three months taking tap-dancing lessons because he admired tap-dancing vaudevillian Pat Rooney, Sr. Now he was doing what he did so well: carefully, systematically getting the better of a tough opponent.

Villon said, "Neon was in on everything in which Milton Connery was involved. I've got no proof, it's all supposition, but I can't think of an alternative scenario, not one that works as good as this one. Mae West told me Neon Light was dying. You name the disease, he had it. Take a number from one to ten. When Neon realized his days were numbered, I suspect he wanted to live it up. He probably didn't have anything stashed away in the bank, and I suspect he wanted a large sum of money to accomplish several things. Money for this anonymous brother who had begged him not to become an impersonator. Money to give himself a joy ride like he'd never known so maybe there'd be some laughs for a kid who'd made others laugh when there was no laughter for him. Damn it, he was only twenty-three years old." Involuntarily he banged his fist on the desk. "Jesus, was there an autopsy?"

"I didn't think it was necessary. God damn it, his skull was bashed in. His brains were spilled."

"Not in Griffith Park. He wasn't killed in Griffith Park. I'll lay dollars to doughnuts he was murdered at the Tailspin Club. Jesus Christ, Felix, do you really sleep at night?"

"Yeah. I sleep at night." He spoke quietly, they didn't miss the irony in his voice. "Why not? There's no one to bother me. I live alone. I got no woman. I never had no woman. All I had was whores. I prefer blondes. Like Mae West is blonde. That kind of blonde. So I retire. What's to look forward to? A couple of beers at the local saloon. A movie. Maybe the burley-Q downtown sometimes. So what? But you see, now I can travel. Now I can get out of this goddamn garbage pail of a city. Buy some new suits. Clean myself up. I'll only be sixty.

That's not so old, is it?'' His voice choked. He was crying. Mallory was uncomfortable. He thought of giving him a friendly pat on the shoulder but he was afraid of contamination.

Villon was all business, seemingly ignoring Dvorack's litany of self-pity. But underneath, he was understanding the man's unhappiness, his desperation for one last laugh, the only thing he had in common with Neon Light. "Jim, get an exhumation order for Neon Light's body and order an autopsy. Maybe that cracked skull wasn't the only reason for his death. And what progress have you made with Miss West's doormen?''

"I've got three nice guys on their way to see her right now. She wants you to know she's crazy about her bodyguards. So are Goneril and Desdemona.''

"Get a move on." Mallory made a rapid exit.

"What happens now?" asked Dvorack.

"Nothing.''

"You ain't blowing the whistle on me?''

"Not yet.''

Dvorack was dumbfounded. "You've got the goods on me.''

"I'll need you when I get the goods on Connery.''

"But I told you I accepted his bribe. Mallory's a witness.''

"That's just a fraction of what I need. Orgies. Hidden cameras. Blackmail. Neon Light. I need a hell of a lot of proof, and I don't know where I'm going to find it and I'm starting looking right now.''

Dvorack said quietly, "Thanks, Herb. I really mean it.''

Villon said nothing. There was nothing to say. Felix Dvorack struggled out of the chair and stumbled to the door. He thought of prison and the revenge that could be exacted on him there. He pulled the door open and walked blindly down the hall. The prospect of an ugly future had shattered him. He found the men's room. He ran past an officer washing his hands and went into an empty stall. He shut the door and latched it.

The officer said, "Glad you made it in time, Felix.''

In the stall, Felix placed his service revolver in his mouth and pulled the trigger. His brains made a colorful pattern on the wall behind him. The officer was in shock. Others poured into the room, including Herb Villon. Villon asked him, "Felix Dvorack?" The officer nodded dumbly. Herb commented, "It shouldn't have come to this."

A few minutes later, Villon was back at his desk. Mallory came in looking as though he'd seen a ghost. "Did you hear? Did you hear what Felix did? What an awful mess. What are you going to tell the chief?"

"What I want him to know."

Mallory sank into the chair Felix Dvorack had recently vacated. "What's the next step with Milton Connery?"

"I give him enough rope."

"Aren't you going to bring him in?"

"Why?"

"Why? For bribing Felix."

"Can we prove it?"

"For crying out loud, Herb, we both heard Felix's confession!"

"We haven't got it in writing. A smart lawyer would shred our testimony if we ever got Connery to trial. We have to sit back and wait until Connery hangs himself."

"But supposing it's a long wait?"

"Unlike Miss Mae West, patience is one of my virtues. When's the autopsy scheduled?"

"The coroner said he'd try to squeeze it in tomorrow. He's got a big waiting list."

"You still got no date for tomorrow night?"

"No. Barbara Stanwyck has other plans and his name's Robert Taylor."

"Miss Stanwyck will regret this one day." Mallory smiled. "Well, Jim, I've got a nice surprise for you. You have someone to escort to the Tailspin tomorrow night."

"Oh, God, I hate blind dates."

"This one isn't blind. It's Mae's sister Beverly."

"Oh my, some days are truly luckier than others. I saw her picture in the *Times* this morning."

"So what's wrong? Mae says her sister's a dead ringer for her."

"A slightly jaded dead ringer."

Villon roared with laughter. His intercom buzzed. His chief said, "Herb! Felix Dvorack's committed suicide!"

Villon said, "And I've lost the one person who could have testified against my prime suspect."

The chief said, "You'll come up with someone else."

"From your mouth to God's ears."

TEN

In Mae West's all-white living room, the queen sat on her throne, her eyes cannily examining the three retired police officers recruited by Jim Mallory. She liked what she saw. They liked what they saw. It was the beginning of a mutual admiration society. Desdemona entered holding a tray that held three steins of beer and a bowl of pretzels. She distributed the beers to the men, who had identified themselves as Timothy Madden, Al Schwartz, and Roscoe Werber.

"Gentlemen," said Mae, "I'm truly glad to meet you. I've always been a fan of cops, retired or otherwise. Now I hope you don't think it's a comedown comin' from police work to taking a job as a doorman. I'd hate to think you think it's beneath you."

Timothy Madden said, "Miss West, the only thing beneath me is the sidewalk."

"Oh, really." She smiled. "You sound like you got the makin's of a gag man. It's Timothy Madden, right?"

"I'm the fourth Timothy Madden with which my family's been blessed." He raised his glass. "Here's mud in your eyes, Miss West." The others joined him in the toast.

"When it comes to slingin' mud, we're in the right town. You got a family, Timothy?"

"There's me wife, Nora, and three daughters and two sons. They're all off on their own. That leaves Nora, me, and the radio. It's a relief to the wife and me that I'll be out of the house part of the day. It'll give us both some breathing space. And the salary Mr. Timothy has promised is quite reasonable. It's not easy making ends meet on the pension we draw." The others murmured assent. "So Mallory's found us at the right time, bless his heart."

Al Schwartz, the smallest but lithest of the three, interjected. "We're old friends, we three. Roscoe here and myself joined the force the same day."

"I was already there," said Timothy with a sweet smile. "Sort of a one-man welcoming committee."

"Ah, Miss West," said Roscoe Werber, "the stories we could tell."

"Not right now," Mae said quickly. "Let's decide who takes which eight-hour shift."

Al Schwartz suggested they do it in alphabetical order. The others agreed. So it was Madden, Schwartz, and Werber, in that order.

Timothy Madden said, "If you boys don't mind, since you're both living on your own being widowers, I'd like to be considered for a daytime shift. I don't like leaving Nora on her own at night. She being bleached blonde and buxom, the vampire killer might mistake her for one of Miss West's impersonators."

Roscoe Werber said flatly, "Not possible," and Timothy shot him a look. "I expect you want us to start right away."

"Yeah, boys, even though I got my bodyguards on the premises, I got my other tenants to consider. They could be in danger too. You never know what to expect from killers. If this here vampire is hyperthyroid, he just might kill anybody out of frustration if he can't get me."

Werber looked at his wristwatch and volunteered to take the first shift at eight P.M. "Then Al can take over at four A.M. And, Timothy, you come in at noon and hold the fort until I resume at eight tomorrow night and so forth and so on."

Mae said, "Of course you boys have gotta have a day off. Well, I can spare one of my muscle boys, I'm sure. They're so young and eager to please, and I'm so eager to be pleased. Now, my girl Goneril will bring down a Thermos of coffee and some sandwiches for you, Roscoe. Say, did you bring any protection for yourselves?" All had brought their service revolvers at Mallory's insistence. Mae smiled. "You boys look like a walkin' armory. That's the way I like it. There's a terlet in the basement for your necessities, and if anything else comes up, you can ring my bell. I'm a light sleeper but a heavy breather." She smiled that smile that they would soon recognize as the one she flashed when she was kidding them. "Drink up, gents, let's not waste good beer. Now if you'll excuse me, my friends are waitin' in the dinin' room. Take your time, boys, there's more beer if you want it. Roscoe, you'll need a clear head."

"Not to worry, Miss West, one beer's my limit."

After exchanging good nights, the men left and Mae joined Jim Timony and Seymour Steel Cheeks in the dining room. "Well, boys, my doormen are lookin' good." Jim was standing behind her chair waiting to seat her. "Thanks, Jim, I like bein' treated like a lady. Oh, look at what Goneril's fixed for the first course, vishy swah and with lots of chives." She spooned some into her mouth. "Terrific. Now, listen, you two. Beverly's train pulls into Pasadena sometime around noon tomorrow. I want you two to take the Rolls and meet her. Y'know, give her the royal treatment she's expectin' to get. I don't know how much luggage she's carryin' but knowin' Beverly, you better be on the safe side and hire a pickup truck to meet you there. I don't know what I'll do when it gets here, the guest bedroom ain't all that big. It was designed for small guests. I'm takin' Desdemona and Goneril with me to the studio in case I have to work late. I know they're dyin' to go to the party at the Tailspin, but I don't know if that's such a good idea."

"Why not, Mae? They deserve a treat every now and then."

"Listen, Jim. You ain't here with them like I am. Their life is one long treat. I'm sure they've both got boyfriends stashed away someplace and I know they both sock their money away for the future. Which is very wise of them. Goneril keeps tryin' to feed me Aunt Jemima pancakes because she keeps buyin' stock in the company. Come to think of it, I ought to look into it myself. Goneril's just bought herself a new fur jacket. Seymour, you've been looking dejected all day. What's eatin' you? Is it the bodyguards?''

"Well, I suppose I should tell you." Mae suspected what was coming. "I'm very concerned about my future." Mae was right.

"You didn't have any future until you met up with me. If I hadn't caught you in the Thanksgiving parade on Hollywood Boulevard, wearin' that sexy loincloth and stalkin' them Pilgrims with your bow and arrow, you'd still be out there with no future. You want to try your luck in pitchers? It's a thought. Like all the rest of them, you ain't got no talent. It's worth settin' up a screen test. You want to do a test?''

"I don't think I'd be very good in the movies. There aren't any good parts for Indians."

"Yeah, but think of it this way. The dialogue's a cinch. 'How,' 'Ugh,' and 'White man speak with forked tongue.' Let me talk it over with my producer, Emmanuel Cohen. Manny's one of the good guys, which is why I have an idea they're soon gonna ease him out."

It wasn't what Seymour wanted to hear. He was obsessed by the word he had heard in the limousine earlier that day after they left the gymnasium. He was obsessed with the word annuity. He didn't know what it meant, but he was savvy enough to know it had something to do with money. Mae had offered Jim an annuity and overrode him when he professed not to want it. Seymour wanted an annuity. He wanted the annuity even more than he wanted to own real estate. It was three years since his father and mother scraped together enough money to send Seymour away from the reservation and out into the world to make his fortune, like his three older brothers before him. The eldest, Irving Steel Cheeks, was making good money in Chicago working in skyscraper construction. Indians were preferred because they were so sure-footed. The next oldest, Louis Steel Cheeks, was a trick rider with a carnival show that toured the country nine months of the year. He was saving his money to buy a ranch in New Mexico. Hymie Steel Cheeks wrote his parents and told them he was doing just great in "trading" up north in Portland, Oregon. "Trading" was a metaphor for housebreaking and robbery. He wrote his baby brother Seymour the truth of his chosen vocation but told him in these sorry economic times, robbery was better than selling his body on the streets. Seymour sought out Los Angeles because his father had read somewhere there were lots of rich women there who would happily sponsor such a magnificent specimen as he. His parents threw a weekend-long festival when Seymour wrote and told them he was being sponsored by the great white star Mae West. Being the good and generous sport that she is, Mae sent his parents some gifts along with a selection of autographed photos of herself. The government agents who monitored the reservation where the Steel Cheeks parents resided were getting a little bored with Mrs. Steel Cheeks's perpetual invitation to "Come up'n see me sometime."

It was while Desdemona was serving coffee and petit fours in the living room that Herb Villon arrived with Jim Mallory. Mae was genuinely delighted to see them. Herb apologized for not phoning ahead but he and Jim, coming from dinner, had cruised by the building, saw Roscoe Weber guarding the door, and stopped to chat with him. Jim explained, "When Roscoe said you were at home, I decided to come up and tell you what happened today." Jim Timony elected to go out on the balcony to smoke a cigar and took with him a snifter of brandy. Seymour volunteered to go to the floor below and see if the bodyguards were comfortable, Mae having voiced some concern. Desdemona fetched demitasse cups for the detectives. After they refused Mae's offer of brandy, Desdemona departed and the three settled down, Mae on her throne chair, Villon and Mallory on a settee. Mallory was tempted by a box of chocolates on an end table and helped himself to one.

Villon told Mae the tragic circumstances of Felix Dvorack's suicide. Mae, one hand on hip, said, "That was kinda sudden, wasn't it?"

Villon said, "It took me by surprise. I hate surprises."

Mae understood. She asked, "So you think maybe Milton Connery's our vampire killer?"

"I don't think that at all," Villon corrected her.

"I must have misheard you. You said you suspected this here Dvorack took a payoff from Connery, so naturally I thought Dvorack had the goods on Connery."

"What Dvorack had, I suspect, was a suspicion that Connery killed Neon Light."

"Why, that dirty dog!" Mae bristled. "That's like killin' the duck that laid the golden egg!"

"That's like also keeping Neon from going public with what he knew about the orgies and the blackmail." Herb explained his theory about Neon possibly wanting the money, partially as a legacy to his brother and partially for a fling he'd never had an opportunity to fling before.

"Yeah," said Mae, "that sounds possible. Neon had all sorts of guilts about his brother. And Neon had all sorts of dreams about seein' Paris and London and Rome and Coney Island. Herb, do you think Neon took part in these orgies?"

"I think so. There are lots of men who find pretty boys dressed in drag as sexually attractive as the real thing."

"The 'lean-back' types," said Mae.

"The 'lean-back' types?" questioned Mallory.

"Yeah. They lean back and say, 'You do what you like, kid. I don't do anythin'.' There's a lot of that goin' on. It's been goin' on for centuries, I'm sure." There was a faraway look in her eyes. "When I was a kid just gettin' goin' in show business, I could have gone bad like Neon did. I was offered plenty of opportunities. I began as a shimmy dancer, you might have heard." Mallory had no idea what a shimmy was. "A shimmy dancer stands in one place and wiggles her hips and her behind real fast, but then she starts slowin' down and soon she's just doin' this." Mae was on her feet, hands outstretched horizontally and sinuously moving her body to the self-accompaniment of "The St. Louis Blues." "You get the idea, boys?" They had gotten more than one idea but neither one had the courage to express them. "Nice to know I'm still up to the shimmy. The greatest was a lady named Gilda Grey. She even made a couple of silent pitchers here at Paramount. With the way she shimmied, she didn't have to be able to talk. She did hers to "I Wish That I Could Shimmy Like My Sister Kate." Y'know, it's funny, Seymour and I went to see the new Jeanette MacDonald and Nelson Eddy musical, *Rose Marie*. There's a scene in some saloon up in Canada, some guy at the piano playin' honky tonk and some gal with a down deep and dirty voice singin' along with the piano and would you believe it, that was Gilda Grey." She shook her head from side to side. "I thought of lookin' her up and then I thought, what's the pernt? Let's get back to business. Herb, you think Connery murdered Neon."

"Or had him murdered."

"But you ain't got the proof, have you? You think he's the vampire?"

"No."

"You're that positive."

"Connery's a slimy bum. The vampire killer's got class."

"Class!" Mae's hands were on the hips, as always when agitated.

"He's got style. He's original. He's got a great imagination."

Mae said through a smile, "He sounds so temptin' I'd like to have him up for dinner some night."

"He just might show up. Uninvited." Villon wasn't smiling. He watched Mae resume her place on the throne chair. "You see, Mae, I have to build myself an imaginary portrait of what I'm up against. Although I haven't seen it for myself, I imagine he works in a cape with a cowl to hide his face."

"A cowl? What cowl? You mean like Jane Cowl, the Broadway star?"

"Cowl as in hood. A hood attached to a cape."

"Well, if you mean hood why don't you say hood? Although come to think of it, had you said 'hood' I might have thought you meant a smalltime crook. Go on, don't let me interrupt too much."

"He has this instrument that simulates fangs. I can't figure out what it is, whether it's on a chain that hangs around his neck or maybe he had a dentist fashion some fangs that he attaches to his teeth."

"Yeah, that's the best idea yet, exceptin' I should think dentists read the newspapers and if they've read about the vampire, the dentist what made these fangs is sure to call you cops and tip you off."

"We haven't had that tip so maybe no dentist was involved. The vampire's too smart for that."

"You make him sound like he's got a college degree."

"He probably does."

"Oh, yeah? He's got class. He's got style. He's got a college degree. What a catch. Well, don't snicker. I don't get many of them intellectuals crossin' my path, and when they do, they don't stop for too long a look. I ain't the kind of gal you can take home to your mother unless your mother's Sophie Tucker. So am I wrong in thinkin' Agnes the witch is mixed up in this someplace?"

"I'd appreciate your remaining very friendly with her."

"Which means you think she's mixed up in this someplace. The poor sap. Y'know, boys, I'm really quite fond of Agnes. If she's gone wrong, I hope she ain't gone too far wrong. I suppose even though she's no erl paintin', that won't keep her from gettin' hung."

"If she's anything, I think she's the go-between who rounds up the participants in the orgies."

"Yeah, Agnes has always expressed this here desire to be a talent scout. And y'know, all these actors and actresses who are probably involved ought to have their heads examined. Better still, they should have their contracts examined. Y'know there's a morals clause in every Hollywood contract. If you step out of line, they can cancel your contract and you'll probably never work again in this town."

Villon asked, "You got one in your contract?"

"Sure I do," she said with a sly smile, "but it was written with invisible ink. Ha! They can try, but they'll never catch me at anythin'. Herb, let me tell you about me in case you haven't already caught on. My act is all a joke, a put-on. I don't smoke, I rarely drink and only then maybe some wine or sherry, and I try to go to church most Sundays. Can't say as I ever get there, but I put in plenty of time tryin'. And that if only for some peace of mind." Jim Timony had returned from the balcony and sat behind Mae, his legs crossed. "As for me, sure there's been men, a steady stream of them when possible, I'm only human. But you know somethin', I ain't really ever known genyoowine love, you know, like that junk they write about in romantic novels. Oh, I've had my crushes and my infatuations but they always canceled each other out. Somethin' always comes up to take my mind off it. Y'see, I'm a narcissist. I just can't love anybody the way I love myself. That's why I can kid myself and kid my audience and give us all a good time while I'm doin' it. When I lose that, I'll retire. Maybe settle in some villa in the south of France like the serial queen Pearl White and learn me some French. Trouble is, to retire is to grow fat, and I'm always havin' to watch my diet. You know the screen puts ten pounds on you, and I don't need any more curves than what I already got. So what happens now, Herb? What's the blueprint?"

"Tomorrow night, we keep our eyes and our ears open. If Milton Connery zeroes in on us, then I'll leave it up to you to enchant him."

"I'd do better with a cobra although there ain't much difference. What about Agnes?"

"Your usual chummy self."

"I got that part down pat, so that won't be a problem. Say, Mallory, you got yourself a date for tomorrow night?"

"I sure do."

"Oh, yeah? Who is she?"

"Her name's Beverly West."

Mae laughed and then said, "Jim, you're a good sport. And you won't know how good a sport you are until you've spent an evening with Beverly. The nicest thing about her is she don't shovel her food on the fork with her thumb." She paused for timing. "She uses her index finger. Timony, I know you're there. You're awful quiet."

"You know I prefer listening to chiming in."

Mae told the detectives, "He's pullin' up stakes and headin' back to civilization soon. I'm gonna miss him."

Timony wished that it was so.

Villon asked Mae, "Mae, did you ever meet Neon's adoptive parents? Their name was Williamson."

"No, I didn't. It's like I told you, Neon sidestepped personal questions. He was pretty quick on his feet where those were concerned. Like I told you before, he cared the most about his older brother, even though he wouldn't give up the impersonatin' the way his brother wanted him to."

Villon now told her, "Mae, I've had Neon's body exhumed."

"Meanin' what?"

"Dug up. It's in the morgue. The coroner's going to perform an autopsy some time tomorrow."

"I know what autopsies are. They're indecent. Cuttin' up a body when it can't fight back."

"I think the autopsy is very necessary. I want to know if maybe he was slipped something before his skull was crushed."

"Slipped something like a Mickey Finn? Something to knock him out?"

"Slipped something like maybe poison. And then the killer, afraid of the possibility of an autopsy, crushed his skull to get us off the scent. There are detectives like Felix Dvorack who'll take a crushed skull at face value and not hunt around for anything else suspicious."

"That poor kid. His life was one pain after another, and now you don't even let him rest in peace. Well, if he was perzoned, why do I get the hunch it might have been with some kind of witches' brew?"

"Anything's possible in an investigation. That's the fun side of detective work."

"I ain't been doin' so bad, have I, Herb?"

"You've been doing great. Head of the class."

"That sounds good and makes me feel good. You hear that, Jim? I'm makin' good again." She said to Villon, "You know what they used to say about me back in New York? 'Local girl makes bad.' " Seymour Steel Cheeks returned from the bodyguards' apartment. "So, Seymour, how're the boys doin'?"

"They're asleep."

"Already?" She looked at her wristwatch. "My my my, how time flies. It's almost eleven o'clock, and I've got an early call at the studio." To the detectives she suggested, "If you're in the vicinity of Paramount Pitchers tomorrow, boys, why don't you drop in and catch some of the shootin'. Film shootin', that is, of course. You know, Paramount's right next door to RKO. Pitchers and right behind us is Hollywood Cemetery. They got Rudolph Valentino there and that dumb kid Virginia Rappe, the one that got killed in the Fatty Arbuckle scandal. He got a real bum Rappe."

"Oh, Mae," admonished Villon.

"I know, I know. It's late and I'm tired." She walked the detectives to the door. "I want to know the result of Neon's autopsy. If I have to change some thinkin' about some people. I got a real heavy day ahead of me tomorrow." She clucked her tongue. "Hallowe'en party. Here's hopin' there ain't too many tricks behind the treats."

ELEVEN

AT EIGHT O'CLOCK THE NEXT MORNING, Mae sat in her exquisite white caravan on the Paramount lot, being fussed over by a hairdresser, a makeup girl, a manicurist, and costume designer Travis Banton while Desdemona and Goneril marveled at how much younger she looked because of these ministrations.

"You're as young as you feel," advised Mae, "and I like to feel young. And I'm gonna start playin' younger parts. Enough of these women of the world. You see this here book I been readin'?" She slapped a palm on the book that rested on her dressing table. "It's all about the Civil War and this here girl Scarlett O'Hara. The book's new. My agent sent it to me to see if I'd be interested in the part of this here whore Belle Watlin'. Well, I ain't interested in playin' no more whores, even if that's what my vast public wants to see me playin'. Now take this here Scarlett O'Hara. She's a real bitch, out to steal some other gal's boyfriend. Anyway, Timony's been readin' the book too and he's been tellin' me most of it as I ain't got much patience with readin' books. Well, if they ever get around to filmin' it, I intend to play Scarlett O'Hara."

Travis Banton blanched. "Mae, with all due respect . . ."

"Which I richly deserve."

"I've read the book. Just about everyone in Hollywood has

111

either read it or is reading it. Scarlett O'Hara is sixteen years old with a seventeen-inch waist.''

''You been around Hollywood a long time, Travis. Shame on you. Ain't you heard of trick photography?''

''I've also heard of miracles.''

Mae smiled at his reflection in the dressing table mirror. ''Whaddya think of my bodyguards?''

''You get them from Central Casting?'' He was fussing with a sleeve that wasn't draping correctly.

''No, honey. Mr. Timony scouted them at Hasseltine's Gym. Ain't they somethin'? Of course I had final approval. Maybe I can work them into the pitcher.''

''As what? Most of it takes place on a farm.''

''Well, farm's got barns, right? And barns got haylofts, right? They could be pitchin' hay in the hayloft till I come in and put a stop to such nonsense and put the three of them to a better use. I might even do a song number with them backin' me up. You gotta admit it's not a bad idea.''

''Mae, it isn't your ideas that are bad, it's your notions.''

An assistant director stuck his head in the door. ''We're ready for you on the set, Miss West.''

''Well, they'll have to wait until I fall into place.'' The sleeve finally satisfied Banton, and Mae examined herself carefully in the mirror. Desdemona and Goneril stood with their arms folded, and Mae asked them, ''Do I meet with your approval?''

Desdemona said, ''I always think you look just fine, Miss West.''

Goneril added, ''But you know what they say, the camera never lies.''

Said Mae as she got to her feet, ''I've known a few cameras I've thought of suin' for perjury. Come on. Let's get the show on the road.'' She led the entourage from the custom-built caravan. Outside, she smiled at her three bodyguards who were on cloud nine, ogling the beautiful extras and starlets. ''Boys, your eyes are bigger than your stomachs. I hope them's your pistols in your pockets.''

A wardrobe mistress was hurrying to Travis Banton. ''Mr.

Banton! Mr. Banton! They need you in wardrobe right away! It's a madhouse! Half the lot's there taking costumes and gowns to wear to Hallowe'en parties tonight!"

Banton followed the wardrobe mistress while Desdemona and Goneril, eyes ablaze at the prospect of joining the looting, went hurrying after them.

Mae said to her bodyguards as they walked the short distance to the sound stage where her movie was shooting, "You're gonna have your work cut out for you tonight, boys. I think there's gonna be an awful lot of Mae Wests out there. I'm beginnin' to worry about that party at the Tailspin." Selma Jefferson Burr held open the heavy iron door, and Mae rewarded him with a warm smile as she led her retinue inside.

Once on the sound stage, Mae was in her element. This was home, this was sanctuary, this was the palace where she was the absolute monarch. She waved at the host of grips, electricians, sound engineers, and other assorted factotums. "Hello, gentlemen," she shouted. "You get much last night? I hope you did. The way contented cows give great milk, contented men do better jobs." She said to the head electrician, "Lots of baby pinks, remember." He indicated the rack of baby pink spotlights overhead, and Mae's thumb and index finger married to signal her approval. Baby pink spotlights were a godsend to middle-aged actresses. She greeted Henry Hathaway, the director, who was better known for his action and adventure films. "Say, Henry, you figure a way to get me on a horse? It might make you feel more at home."

Hathaway responded with a brusque "Good morning."

Mae tolerated him. She hadn't wanted him on the film, but Emmanuel Cohen had pleaded with her to accept him as he'd been without an assignment for over a month, and movie studios wanted their contract personnel to work continuously. Even their most important actors made as many as four or five features a year; directors were known to accomplish five or six. Mae greeted Randolph Scott, one of her leading men, and as she looked at his handsome face, which was occupied with a buttered roll, she wondered if the gossip about him and his housemate, Cary Grant, was true. She'd given Grant his first big break as her leading man in *She Done Him Wrong* and then used him again in her third film, *I'm No Angel*. Well, she decided, if they're a hot and heavy, who could blame them, they're both so gorgeous.

Elizabeth Patterson, the character actress playing Randolph Scott's mother, apprehended Mae, showing her the morning's *Los Angeles Times*. "Have you seen this, Mae?" It was a story of Neon Light's exhumation and the possibility his murder was connected to the vampire killings. "Doesn't all this notoriety frighten you?" The bodyguards recognized her and surrounded her, beaming like klieg lights at a grand opening at Grauman's Chinese Theater.

"No, Elizabeth. It don't frighten me one bit. And this here vampire killer don't frighten me either. Meet my three gorgeous bodyguards." She introduced them. "Well, Elizabeth, don't you wish you were thirty years younger?"

The older actress laughed. "Mae, I wouldn't know what to do with them if I was."

"You'd know, all right, honey, you'd know. You'd do what all of us do, you just let nature take its course. Anything in the paper about the suicide of a detective named Felix Dvorack?"

"It's in the article about the exhumation. He was this Neon Light's investigator, you know, investigating his murder."

Mae borrowed the newspaper and skimmed the article. "Why, the dirty so-and-sos. Nothin' about me bein' the reason they're givin' Neon a comeback. Y'know, I knew the poor kid. It was me what suspected there was a connection between Neon and the three vampire killin's."

Miss Patterson clasped her hands and said sincerely, "This killer's a maniac. Nothing must happen to you, Mae."

"Oh, something's got to happen to me, Elizabeth, I'm the restless type. I can't sit still for too long. And I don't take nothin' lyin' down unless he's attractive, y'know what I mean?"

"Oh, Mae, don't you ever take anything seriously?"

"Sure. My weekly paycheck." She chucked the older actress under the chin. "You're a great gal, Elizabeth. And I appreciate your worryin' about me." She took the actress by the arm and led her to the dressing room provided for her on the set, outside of which was a table and chairs, the table set with fine china and silverware and groaning with coffee, tea, cocoa, assorted pastries, rolls, jams, jellies, cheeses, butter, and a deck of cards. "But, y'know, there's a special God what watches over me. At least I think there is. This here vampire ain't gonna sink his fangs into my neck unless I invite him to, and that's not very likely." She guided the actress to a chair and sat next to her. "Besides, I got two smart detectives on this nut's tail. They might show up on the set today. I'll introduce you. You'll like them, I think. They're Herb Villon and Jim Mallory. Terrific go-getters. My money's on them. What are you havin', Elizabeth?"

"Nothing special. I'll just pick."

Mae looked around annoyed. She motioned to a buxom blonde young woman, Billie Doux, the production secretary. "Say, Billie. You seen Desdemona and Goneril? They're never around when I need them."

"I just left them in wardrobe." She was chewing gum while studying the tray of pastries hungrily. "They're looking for something to wear tonight, just like everybody else. They said they were going to the party at the Tailspin."

"Oh, brother, that's all I need. Well, they've got the night off, they can do as they please. For cryin' out loud, Billie, pick one already if you don't give a damn about your figure."

"To hell with my figure," said Billie as she chose a cheese danish, "when I'm hungry I eat. Otherwise I get very cranky." She bit into the pastry with a ferocity that made Mae cringe. As she chewed she said, "I'll be at the Tailspin myself. You'll die when I tell you who I'll be dressed up as."

"Then don't tell me. I like to think I've got a lot of good years ahead of me."

"Amen to that," said Miss Patterson as she wished the director would get a move on and shoot a scene.

Billie Doux giggled and said, "I'm going as Mae West in *She Done Him Wrong!*"

Mae groaned. "Can't you think of something original? I'm gonna be up to my hips in Mae West impersonators tonight. I'm takin' a party to the Tailspin tonight and probably nobody'll recognize me because I ain't wearin' no costume."

Elizabeth Patterson was genuinely concerned. "Now, you listen to me, Billie Doux. There's a murderer out there killing Mae West impersonators. You're putting yourself in danger!"

"Aw, booshwah! He's been killing professionals. I'm just a nice chubby civilian. I do a great impersonation of you, Miss West."

Mae said wearily, "It seems so does everybody except Queen Marie of Romania and I ain't really too sure about her." Her mouth froze. "Goneril! Just who the hell are you suppose to be!"

Honk!

Goneril wore an orange, curly wig. She had on a frayed checked jacket and baggy trousers. She carried a prop car horn, which she honked with maniacal frenzy. "Don't you recognize me? I'm Harpo Marx!"

"Unbelievable," Mae whispered to herself, "unbelievable."

"Falling in love againnnnnn . . ."

Desdemona had come in behind Mae and Elizabeth Patterson. She carried a chair, placed it in front of Mae, put one not too shapely leg on it, and baritoned Marlene Dietrich's signature song. Her stockings were rolled into a knot just below her knees. The theatrical skirt she wore exposed more thigh then anyone could stomach. On one thigh she sported a bright red garter. Her blouse revealed an amount of cleavage that would have driven a drunk to signing the pledge. All activity on the set had stopped dead.

Mae asked Billie Doux, "Honey, you got any smellin' salts?"

Milton Connery had read the item about Neon's exhumation and the news of Felix Dvorack's suicide. He phoned Agnes Darwin, who had not yet read the newspaper. When she heard what the article contained, she said with her customary good sense, "They've got nothing on us."

116

"I wish I could be as sure as you are."

"If they did, we'd both be downtown in the precinct by now screaming for lawyers."

"They could be playing games with us. Villon's the type, I can tell he is."

Agnes thought for a moment. "If he is, Mae will know. I think I'll drop in on her at the studio, see if I can find out anything."

"Don't be too obvious. Mae has a very suspicious nature."

"When have I ever been obvious?"

"I'll let that one pass. I'm going to lay low for a while on the special parties." "Special parties" was his coy appellation for orgies.

This annoyed Agnes. "Why? Dvorack knew nothing about them. The only one who was a threat was Neon and he's dead."

"No, he's not. He's alive again. Read the article for yourself. He's getting an autopsy. I'm sure that's Villon's doing. Villon suspects it wasn't just the crack on the skull that finished off Neon."

"Oh, God."

"Don't count on God for any help. Use your bean, Agnes. Why do you suppose Dvorack croaked himself? Villon must have accused him of taking money to put the kibosh on the Neon case. Villon must have squeezed the truth out of him."

Agnes ran fingers through her hair. She was getting agitated. "Then he knows it's you."

"If he does, he hasn't been around to see me and it's a long time after breakfast."

"Then you agree. They've got nothing on us."

"You think Dvorack was thoughtful enough to croak himself to keep from fingering me?"

"Detectives are rarely thoughtful. Listen, Milton. Even if Dvorack did blow the whistle, he's dead. It's your word against a dead man's. Villon knows that."

"He might have it in writing."

"If he did, he'd be standing next to you."

"You're right. You're a damned smart witch, Agnes."

"So how come I'm still single?"

Simon LeGrand, the club manager, stood on the dance floor in the center of the club surveying his handiwork with self-satisfaction. Every decoration was artfully in place. The large room was a Grand Guignol of Halloween decor. He clasped his hands together and cried, "I am so damn proud of myself!" He then stretched his arms out to the several people who had helped him decorate the room. "Each and every one of you deserves an Academy Award for your delicious contributions. I could kiss each and every one of you on the lips!" Almost everyone cringed. "This shall go down in my memory book as one of my most memorable accomplishments."

He heard Milton Connery bellowing "Jesus Christ! The place looks like a fucking kindergarten!"

"I shall *spit!*"

Jim Timony and Seymour Steel Cheeks stood on the platform watching the *Twentieth Century Limited* pulling in. As the train slowed down, the engine exhaled a cloud of steam that enveloped the two men. The train ground to a halt with an agonizing screeching of brakes. A porter stepped on to the platform and placed a sturdy box under the steps leading down from the car. He held up his hand and it was firmly grasped by Beverly's, her rings sparkling in the cruelly bright California sunshine. Timony said to Seymour, "I've never seen paste sparkle so beautifully." Beverly stepped onto the platform and Timony heard Seymour gasp. He had never seen her before. Her resemblance to Mae was uncanny. She was wearing one of Mae's cast-off Chanels, a cleverly designed affair meant to be worn at a garden party. She wore a large picture hat decorated with cloth peonies and gardenias. She was a perfect carbon copy of her celebrated sister. Timony planted a kiss on her cheek. Beverly was sizing up Seymour Steel Cheeks. Timony could hear her purring with approval.

"And I suppose this is Chief Sittin' Bull?" She held out a hand to Seymour. "How," Beverly greeted in a voice dripping with molasses. Seymour was paralyzed. This couldn't be Mae.

She was at the studio. But the voice. It was Mae's voice. His skin crawled. Beverly patiently continued to pose with her hand outstretched. She said in an aside to Timony, "Don't he know he's supposed to kiss my hand? If he don't, Mae ain't trained him right." Awkwardly Seymour took her hand. His lips brushed the hand. The perfume. Mae's perfume, her favorite, created especially for her in Paris by a Spanish emigré: *Noche de Diablo*. The Devil's Night. Now the hands were on her hips. Just like Mae. "A pussy got your tongue? What's your name?"

"Seymour Steel Cheeks."

"Well, I'm Beverly. I'm sure we're gonna be real good friends."

Timony said, "Beverly, that can't possibly be all your luggage." There were almost twenty pieces including two wardrobe trunks that Mae used to use when she toured in her plays.

"I was thinkin' of packin' more but I didn't want to look pretentious. Oh, I see you brought the Rolls. Mae knows how to treat me good. What's that filthy truck for?"

"Your luggage."

Beverly took Seymour's arm and he walked her to the Rolls. "You're shakin' like a leaf." She smiled. "Am I that overwhelmin'?"

"Beverly, lay off," cautioned Timony.

"I ain't gonna hurt him." She said to Seymour, "You ain't afraid of me, are you, Seymour?"

"I'm not afraid."

"Then why's your voice shakin'?" She squeezed his arm. "We're gonna be good friends, Seymour. Real good friends." She released his arm, which freed him to find his handkerchief and mop his brow. Beverly had taken Timony's arm. "Say, Jim, they caught this vampire yet?"

"No, he's still elusive and still very dangerous. He killed a woman the night before last." She showed no reaction. "She'd been doing her impersonations at a private party."

"Say, listen, how does this guy know where to find his

victims? How did he know she'd be doin' a private party? How did he know where to track down the two boys?"

"There are just two agents in this town who represent female impersonators. It's easy to phone and find out who's appearing where and when. It's easy for him to say 'I'd like to book Nedda Connolly for such and such a date.' And he's told that's just fine, she's doing such and such tonight or tomorrow night or whenever and then he says 'I'll phone you to confirm my booking' and then he knows where to find Nedda Connolly. In her case, he found out where she lived and just waited there until she came home."

"Nedda Connolly. She was one of the few women doin' Mae. Is Ruth Gillette still doin' her?"

"I don't think so. Haven't heard of her in a long while."

"Well, I'll soon have the field to myself at the rate this vampire's movin'. Mae's in danger, ain't she?"

"And so are you, unless you decide to cancel tomorrow night and leave town."

"Jim, you know us Wests ain't quitters. Mae's not afraid of the competition, is she?"

"Beverly, there's only one Mae West. You can look like her and you can talk like her, but you haven't got that unique style and charisma that belongs to her and only to her."

"Oh, I think I do pretty good. Don't you agree, Sittin' Bull?"

Seymour didn't reply. He smiled enigmatically and Beverly was satisfied. He walked past her and Timony to the pickup truck and told the driver and his helper to collect Beverly's luggage. Then he got behind the wheel of the Rolls and revved the motor. Once Timony and Beverly were settled in the back-seat, he took off.

Annuity.

He wondered if Beverly had an annuity. Mae had to be supporting her. He knew Mae had a list of charity cases to whom she happily played Lady Bountiful. Old friends fallen on hard times in these hard times. Punch-drunk prizefighters, retired lovers, and at least one ex-con he'd heard her mention.

I've got to get an annuity.

The coroner sat in Villon's office with Herb and Jim Mallory. He was glad to escape his grim venue if only momentarily. He held a cup of steaming black coffee while Villon read his neatly typed report on Neon Light's autopsy following its quick exhumation.

"What's oleandrin?"

"A poisonous juice distilled from the oleander plant."

"I've never come across it before. I'm usually up against cyanide and rat poison, run-of-the-mill stuff like that."

"Oleandrin is very exotic. It must have been administered by someone who's a very original thinker. In a drink like Coca-Cola, for example, the victim would never detect the taste. This is excellent coffee."

"I brew it myself," said Villon, pleased. He indicated a hot plate and a coffeepot. "Coffee's my special blend. I get it at a place in Chinatown. Would you like some?"

"That would be nice, Herb. Have you come across oleandrin before?"

"Just once, which is why I greeted it today like a long-lost friend. The first time around was, oh, let me think, some five or six years ago. Woman poisoned her husband. Beverly Hills. Very posh. Insurance thing. I went nuts trying to figure out what it was that killed him. It was certainly a toxic substance, but which one? I have a friend in Mexico City who's a poison specialist. He tracked it down for me. We talked on the phone at great length. He was curious about the case. I told him the couple were Amanda and Douglas Harbor. He was a tax specialist. She was a hatcheck girl. The husband was some thirty years older than Amanda and very well off. Amanda was a greedy girl, she's serving life now. I asked him how she could have heard of oleandrin, let alone get her hands on it. He said once you've got the oleander plant you just squeeze out the juices and you're in business."

121

"There's a weird place on Fairfax Avenue that carries oleanders, or at least it did then. It's called the Witches' Brew."

"I've heard of it."

"Ever been there?" Villon said he hadn't. "I dropped in one
day just out of curiosity. It's run by a creep named Dwight
Pratt. He's a self-styled warlock. That's a male witch, in case
you didn't already know. He's got the sort of paraphernalia
there that would make a horror film fan's mouth water."

"I wonder if he's got something there that might make my
mouth water."

"Such as?"

"Vampire's fangs."

The coroner said, "It's worth a look. He's got a very original
inventory. Well, I'd better get back to my carving." Mallory
showed a look of distaste. "Thanks for the coffee. If you need
anything else, feel free."

Villon remembered something. "Wait a minute. You did the
vampire victim autopsies too?"

"But of course," he said with exaggeration. "I've got a mo-
nopoly on them."

"I'd like to see those reports again. Maybe you can save me
time if you remember. Were there toxic substances left by the
fangs?"

"No, and I gave the idea a lot of attention. It was the knife
to the heart that did it. And you know, I sort of have this feeling
there's something symbolic about the fangs and the knife to the
heart."

Villon was very interested. "In what way symbolic?"

"Remember back in the early days of silent pictures?"

"I was a kid but I remember."

"All those lady vamps, Theda Bara, Nita Naldi, Rosemary
Theby. Vamps as in vampire. That's the origin of the expression 'vamp.' I've been playing with this theory that the killer is
saying the fang marks represent a woman, a vamp. And the
thrust of the knife to the heart, well, don't laugh. I think it's a
deadly metaphor for killing a vamp with a good heart." He
laughed. "Am I too far out?"

"No. It sounds good to me. Thanks, Doc, thanks a lot."

After the coroner left, Mallory took his place in the chair. "A vamp with a good heart. There's no such thing."

"Yes there is, and her name is Mae West."

TWELVE

"WELL, WELL, WELL," SAID MAE AS she saw Agnes Darwin come into view, "it looks like it might be standin' room only around here soon. Here's Herb Villon and Jim Mallory. They been entertainin' me with some excerpts from Neon Light's autopsy." Agnes exchanged greetings with the detectives, not completely masking the strain she was under since her phone conversation with Milton Connery. "Desdemona, a chair for Miss Darwin. Agnes, I thought you'd be busy at the Tailspin today, what with tonight's big bash."

"Simon LeGrand has everything under control so I've got the day to myself." She sat and searched in her handbag for the inevitable pack of cigarettes. "Oh, there's Warren William. He's one of my favorites."

"Agnes, you're a bundle of nerves."

"I am?"

"You oughta know. It's your bundle."

"I feel perfectly fine." She dropped the pack of cigarettes. Mallory picked them up and handed them to her. "Thank you."

A manicurist was touching up one of Mae's fingernails. "I thought bein' that it's Hallowe'en, your national holiday, you'd be busy at home over a hot kettle."

"The day is unimportant. It's the night that counts."

"My very sentiments," said Mae. "Herb, is this autopsy report a secret document, or can I let Agnes in on some of it?"

"You can let her in on all of it."

Mae said to Agnes, "A rare specimen, a generous detective. Agnes, the autopsy shows that Neon was perzoned."

"But I thought the blow to his skull killed him."

"That's what his killer wanted the cops to think. And that's what they thunk . . . is there such a word?" Villon shrugged. Mallory was grinning. "Well, if there ain't, there is now." She smiled at them, vastly enjoying herself and Agnes's discomfort. "Anyway, Agnes, there was this crooked detective, Felix Dvorack, assigned to Neon's case. The boys here"—she indicated the detectives—"suspected Dvorack was paid off by the killer to squelch the whole thing, which he did. He might have gotten away with it if I hadn't suggested to the boys that Neon's murder might have something to do with the three victims the vampire's knocked off. Well, they confronted Dvorack and the poor son of a gun bumped himself off. So that proves he got paid to do a coverup. What was the name of that perzon again?"

"Oleandrin," said Villon.

"Yeah. That's it. Not as famous as arsenic, but just as effective. It comes from a flower. Imagine, somethin' as pretty as a flower has juices that kill. I don't know why I'm so surprised. I love mushrooms, but you gotta be careful you don't eat any perzoned ones. And that goes for boyfriends too. Ow!" The manicurist apologized. "That's enough, dear. If I've gotten to the pernt where my audiences are interested in my fingernails, then I'm out of business." The manicurist reluctantly gathered up her paraphernalia and left. "Take it from me, she can't wait to spread this conversation to the rest of the studio. I tell you, gossip in this town is like an epidemic. Oh, well, I ain't said much that they can't read in the gazettes." There was a pause as Agnes ground out the cigarette under the sole of her shoe. "The coroner said he only came across it once before in his experience. Some bimbo perzoned her husband for his insurance. You tell her, Herb. I forgot their names."

"I'm sure you remember the case," said Villon. "It happened a few years back."

"The coroner said it was more like five or six years ago," corrected Mallory.

Villon shrugged. "What's a couple of years more or less?"

"Tell that to a woman," commented Mae. "Right, Agnes?" Agnes said nothing. She seemed frozen in position, staring at Villon. Mae sensed Villon had struck a nerve. She looked at him but his eyes were glued to Agnes's face, a cat about to ambush a canary.

Villon resumed talking. "A woman named Amanda Harbor poisoned her husband, Douglas. He was a very wealthy tax consultant."

"Probably as shady as they come," Mae said matter-of-factly. "The kind I wish I had doin' my taxes. Sorry if I derailed you, Herb, my mind's like a Mexican jumpin' bean, it's all over the place."

"She poisoned him with oleandrin. It puzzled the coroner, who's a pretty smart guy, when he did Harbor's autopsy. But a friend in Mexico City came up with the answer. Very exotic poison. It doesn't surface very often. As you gather, hard to identify. In your career as a witch, have you come across it? I mean, I'm sure you work with all kinds of obscure, exotic materials. They probably come in handy when you're concocting a spell."

Agnes was lighting another cigarette. "You should talk to Dwight Pratt. He owns the Witches' Brew on Fairfax. I think I mentioned it to you the other day. He would know about exotic, unusual poisons."

Mae said, "This here Amanda used to work as a hatcheck girl. Say, do you suppose she might have worked at the Tailspin?"

Agnes exhaled a perfect smoke ring. "There's a big turnover in hatcheck girls at the Tailspin. She might have worked there. Amanda Harbor." She paused. "It doesn't ring a bell."

126

"It's not supposed to. It's supposed to jog your memory."
Mae was impatient. She was sure, as she supposed Villon was
sure, that Amanda Harbor might have been employed at the
Tailspin. Five or six years ago, Agnes was already involved with
Milton Connery. And Mae assumed that therefore she spent a
lot of time at the club. Agnes repeated Amanda Harbor's name.
"Harbor was her married name. If she worked there, it was
under her maiden name. You know, like Amanda Smith or
Amanda Jones or maybe Amanda Vorkapich." She smiled
slyly at the detectives. "There's a kid in special effects called
Slavko Vorkapich. How's that for a jawbreaker? What do you
say, Agnes, get the gray cells working."

"What does her working at the Tailspin have to do with
Neon's murder?"

Mae's impatience was at a boil. "What have you got between
your ears, Agnes? Cottage cheese? Neon is perzoned by the
same stuff she fed her husband. Where does some ordinary
former hatcheck girl hear about something like . . . like what?"

"Oleandrin," supplied Villon.

"Yeah, olewhateverthehell. The same thing that killed Neon.
Damn it, Herb, it's dollars to doughnuts the bimbo worked the
Tailspin. Somebody connected with the Tailspin got her the
stuff because she knew it was available at the witch store."

Agnes was aghast. Mae would look back on it as a brilliant
spur-of-the-moment performance. "Mae! How dare you!"

"Depends on what you think I'm darin'."

"You're insinuating it was me that familiarized this Amanda
person with the poison. And you're insinuating I had something to do with killing Neon!"

"Now, ladies," cautioned Villon, "this accidental get-to-
gether is starting to get out of hand." He directed his words at
Mae, and she got his message. Use a soft pedal.

"I'm sorry, Agnes. I didn't mean to get you all hot under the
collar. But all of a sudden it's startin' to get to me. I'm surrounded with murder, new murders and old murders, and it
ain't pleasant. I get tired of listenin' to innuendo and out the

other." She said in an aside to Mallory, "That's an old one but it's always effective."

Agnes was off and running. "I don't remember any Amanda anything working at the Tailspin. I had little to do with the hired help."

"Not very democratic of you, Agnes." Mae wasn't about to let her off the hook.

"Come off it, Mae. We've been good friends for a long time, but your behavior and your insinuations are unbecoming. And, Mr. Villon, I had nothing to do with Neon's death, and frankly, I find it insulting in suddenly being put in the position of defending myself for no damned good reason."

Villon smiled. "You haven't been accused of anything, Miss Darwin, so why do you say you've been forced to defend yourself?"

Agnes bristled. "If you have a suspect, why don't you tell me who it is?"

"That isn't the way we detectives work. We're like bricklayers. We have to build our suspicions slowly, brick by brick. And we only share our information with each other, except for the occasional rodent who can be bought. You knew Felix Dvorack, didn't you?"

"I did not. I know he questioned Milton Connery about Neon, but that's logical as Milton was Neon's manager."

"And it's logical that you knew Neon."

"Of course I did. Mae knows that."

"Did you like Neon?" Mae was wondering, while listening to the give and take between Villon and Agnes, what was taking the director so long in setting up her next scene.

Agnes thought for a moment as she fumbled for a cigarette. "I neither liked nor disliked him. I really can't say. We didn't talk much on the occasions we were together. Neon wasn't a very exhilarating conversationalist. He might have been with others, but never with me."

"Was he trying to blackmail Connery?"

Agnes looked as though she had been shot. Mae was beginning to feel sorry for her. She came to visit, never expecting to end up on a hot seat. But that, as a fortune-teller once told her, is the unexpected twists and turns of fate. Villon repeated the question.

Agnes looked and sounded composed. Mae wondered if she had ever acted professionally. "If he was, I knew nothing about it. But why would he want to blackmail his own manager, the man running his career?"

"Maybe it's because the man has long been suspected of running other things besides Neon's career and the Tailspin Club." Agnes made no comment. "You knew and I'm sure still know Connery very intimately. You had to know the things he was involved in behind the scenes. Of course, all this is hearsay, but it's common gossip in this town that he's been setting up orgies for the sheer purpose of taking pictures of celebrities with hidden cameras and then blackmailing the poor saps."

Agnes snapped each word. "And where are these orgies supposed to have taken place?"

"Various homes rented for the occasion. I'm sure you know real estate values have hit rock bottom due to the depression. It's very easy to rent a house for the night. It's very easy to hire a specialist to rig the house with hidden cameras."

"I don't know anything about things like that!"

Mae drawled, "Aw, come on, Agnes, witches know about everything. Don't witches take part in orgies? I thought that was one of the big enticements in bein' a witch. My good friend Dorothy Parker once told me some publisher named Horace Liverright used to hold orgies in his penthouse back in the mid-twenties. He was always askin' Mrs. Parker to join in, but she refused because she said she wouldn't know which way to turn. Too bad I didn't know her then. I could have given her some useful pernters." She winked at Mallory and the blood rushed to his face. In the dressing room, Goneril and Desdemona were overhearing the conversation with delight.

"I repeat," Agnes said firmly, "I don't know anything about things like that."

Villon was thinking, In a court of law she'd be one hell of a witness for the defense.

Agnes wasn't finished. "Have you any proof of these allega-tions, Mr. Villon?"

"I said it was all hearsay."

"When you have solid proof, Mr. Villon, tell me about it. I find it curious that as intimate as I have been with Milton Connery, I've heard nothing about orgies and photographs and blackmail."

"Now, why don't we all calm down?" suggested Mae. "Goneril! Go find out what's holdin' up the works around here. My makeup's beginnin' to melt and I'm gettin' as restless as a bimbo in a men's club. Where you goin', Agnes?"

Agnes was on her feet. "Frankly, I need some fresh air. I'm sure I'll see you at the club tonight."

"You'll see all of us." Mae's tone of voice changed. "We didn't mean to ruffle your pretty feathers, Agnes. I know you dropped by for some socializin' and didn't expect to get jumped the way you did. But that was just a stroke of fate. You probably saved Herb here some time."

"You did, Miss Darwin. I was intending to have a talk with you."

"Well, you certainly had it," responded Agnes.

"Not as much as I would have liked. There'll be another time."

Agnes Darwin stared at him for a moment then turned on her heel and stalked out of the sound stage.

"Somethin' tells me we have come to the end of a beautiful friendship," said Mae. "Too bad she got mixed up with a bum like Connery, but then, all of us girls have our Achilles' heel, and I've been mixed up with enough heels to prove it. Poor Agnes. Her head's too big for her body and her tongue's too big for her mouth."

"Not this afternoon it wasn't," said Villon.

Mae crossed her legs. "Herb, you're blind. She's still carryin' the torch for Connery. If it was me, I'd shove it under his rear end. Agnes ain't the greatest looker in the world, but she has style. I can see where she could interest a rat like Connery. Agnes is different. She ain't the sort of stuff I'm sure Connery was used to. Cigarette girls, hatcheck girls, and why don't you ask Connery if he remembers a chick named Amanda Something?"

"I intend to."

"She mentioned this here Simon LeGrand. Now I remember the name. He was a friend of Neon's. He's some sort of a manager at the Tailspin. Neon said he's all over the place. You have to catch him with a butterfly net. I'm sure we can have him paged tonight. I know he'll be delighted to meet me." She picked imaginary lint from her dress. "I'm sure he'll remember this Amanda person if she ever worked there. And if she did, five'll get you twenty she learned about that perzon from the witch. And if the same perzon did Neon in, then I'm not too sad about the end of a beautiful friendship. What happens to Agnes if you can prove she provided the perzon both times?"

"It'll be very unpleasant for her."

"Oh, yeah? Maybe she better try to keep on my good side, although all my sides are good. If she gets sent to Alcatraz or San Quentin, I can always have Goneril bake her a cake with a chisel inside."

"What was that about a cake?" asked Goneril, having found out what the delay was with Mae's next scene.

"Never mind about the cake. What's goin' on over there?"

"They's got a problem lighting the set. And it's those bags under Mr. William's eyes."

"Well, why don't they just check them bags someplace and let's get on with it? I need time to prepare for the party. And, oh God, Beverly must be in the apartment by now." She saw the assistant director hurrying her way. "What's goin' on?"

"Sorry about the delay, Miss West. Mr. Hathaway apologizes. It's been solved. We're ready now."

"My makeup needs freshenin' up."

The assistant shouted, "Makeup!"

Mae covered her ears. "Don't yell like that. You're hurtin' my eardrums." The makeup girl arrived, studied Mae's face with her practiced eye, murmured something about Mae needing more number eight, while Mae saw Villon signaling Mallory it was time they left.

"Mae, we'll see you at nine at the Tailspin."

Mae said, "Thanks for comin' by with the autopsy report. It makes me know you've got some kind of respect and admiration for me. I'm glad Agnes showed up too, not for her sake but for yours. What are you goin' to do about Milton Connery?"

"We'll wait until after the witch strikes some fear into his heart. I'm sure she's gone straight to him to tell him what happened here."

Mae said, "I'm still wonderin' if maybe he's the vampire."

"Mae, he's not the vampire. I'm positive he murdered Neon Light."

"Then why don't you bring him in?"

"No proof, beautiful, I've got no proof. All I can do is wear him and Agnes down until, with any luck, they break apart at the seams. But that still leaves me without a vampire to call my own."

The makeup girl said, "There. You're as good as new."

"Honey, I'm always as good as new. By the way, how's that no-good husband of yours?"

"Who? Oh, him." She sighed. "Very bad. Very bad. The doctors say he's lost his mind."

"Well, for your sake, dear, let's hope he doesn't find it. So long, boys!" Mae sauntered away slowly, her mind dwelling on Agnes Darwin and Milton Connery, when she knew she should mentally be going over her lines. Agnes Darwin troubled her more than Milton Connery did. What makes a smart gal like Agnes go wrong? She was no beauty. She always worried about being flat-chested. Mae had advised her wisely that men do not live by breasts alone. Yet Agnes had remarkable assets. She had class, she had poise, she had wit of a sort, and she was a witch. Mae reminded herself she too was some kind of a witch. She had cast many a spell in her day and expected to cast many more.

"Ready, Mr. Hathaway?" asked the assistant director.

"Let's go," said Henry Hathaway. "Okay, Mae?"

"I will be when I feel the heat of them baby pinks."

Hathaway shouted for the baby pinks. In a few seconds they were aglow. Mae took her position on a couch, arranging herself so that she looked as amusingly seductive as her audiences expected her to be. Warren William took his position standing over her.

Mae said sweetly, "Warren, you're in my light."

And he knew no one steps into Mae West's light.

"Well, I suppose it'll do." Beverly was in the all-white guest room, which Jim Timony reminded her was far more comfortable than a hotel room. "There ain't enough room for my luggage."

"After you unpack, we'll store the trunks in the basement."

"There ain't enough room for my things." She opened a closet door. "Ummm, a walk-in. Well, that's a help. How big's the other closet?"

"Same size."

"You must know it well," said Beverly with a sly smile. "I have a feelin' this was once your room."

"I don't deny it. I've spent many a night here."

"You havin' trouble with my sister?"

He told her about his decision to move back East. "Once this vampire killer is caught."

"Supposin' he's too smart to get caught? Then whaddya do?"

"They'll catch him. He's bound to slip up." Seymour Steel Cheeks and the pickup truck driver were struggling into the room with her luggage.

Beverly folded her arms. There was a strange look on her face. "I suddenly feel cold. Is it cold in here?"

"It's over ninety degrees outside."

"I'm cold. Jim, all kiddin' aside, Mae's in real danger, ain't she?"

"Very real danger. You know she's been getting these frightening phone calls."

"Yeah, that's what I'm talkin' about." Murderin' her impersonators is kind of a warm-up for the big number, ain't it?"

133

"That's the threat Mae's living with. We and the police are convinced it's someone who wants her dead."

Beverly sat at the dressing table. "At the Tailspin, he could confuse me for Mae, couldn't he? I could be a marked woman. I don't like the thought of gettin' killed. I got a lot of good years ahead of me."

"If you're frightened, I'll cancel the engagement."

"I ain't chickenin' out. I need this date, Jim. It's no fun livin' in reflected glory. I don't want to spend the rest of my life imitatin' my sister. But what do I do? I got no special talent. I can't write or paint or compose music. I have a rough time with guys lookin' for one, who wants me for me alone and not because with me he can pretend he's sleepin' with Mae West. When I was a kid I slept with Mae West." She snorted. "Big deal. I had ambitions when I was a kid. Mae used to listen to me and encourage me, I've got to give her that."

"Mae is very good to you."

"Don't I know it? Don't I appreciate it? Don't I hate it? Well, it ain't right for me to knock the annuity she gave me."

Seymour Steel Cheeks was on his way out to get the rest of Beverly's luggage. *Annuity.* There it is again. Annuity. I've got to have an annuity.

Beverly removed the picture hat and tossed it on the bed. "It ain't all that great livin' a hand-me-down life." She stared at her reflection in the mirror. "The years are catchin' up on me, Jim. They're catchin' up on Mae too. Does it worry her, Jim?"

"Beverly, don't you know by now that Mae considers herself indestructible?"

"Oh, yeah? Well, has somebody told that to this here vampire killer?"

She picked up a brush and attacked her hair vigorously. Jim Timony walked slowly to a window and looked out at the deserted street. Nobody walked in Hollywood, sidewalks were a redundancy. Beverly's words echoed in his ears. Does the killer really think he'll succeed in murdering Mae?

He said, "You know, Beverly, you're right. It is a little chilly in here."

THIRTEEN

SIMON LEGRAND WAS BEHIND THE BAR, artistically gluing tinsel to the mirror, humming "Stormy Weather" under his breath, dreading the coming of night. Hallowe'en. All those fagots running amok without a license. All the screaming and yelling and the falling-down drunks and the tears and the arguments and bottles flying and glasses flying. And the getups, the bizarre getups. Mardi Gras time. All that would be missing were the floats. Mae West must be out of her mind reserving a table for tonight of all nights. She needs this place two nights in a row like she needs a third tit. He let fly a few choice epithets under his breath. Two nights in a row of madness and mayhem and murder.

Murder?

Simon stared at his reflection. It came to him like the snapping of a finger. Murder. It's been two days since the last one. Nedda Connolly. Nice lady. No trouble ever. No trouble ever again. She's gone. Larry Hopkins and Danny Turallo are gone. Nice boys. No temperament. Good performers. All they asked out of life was applause and a decent fee. Neon Light. So sweet. So innocent. So naive. If there was a dark side to him, Simon had never seen it. Who would want to murder him? Why? He knew there was a brother someplace who didn't like Neon's profession. But so what? Simon had three older brothers who didn't like Simon, but again, so what? He was humming "Star Dust." He always hummed it when he was feeling melancholy. Thinking of Neon always filled him with melancholia. Could Connery have murdered Neon? Something's up. Simon had read the morning paper, about the exhumation, Dvorack's suicide. He remembered Dvorack. The detective had questioned Simon about Neon. He also questioned Connery. Then all of a sudden, no more questions, no more investigation. He said aloud, "Very, very fishy."

"What's very, very fishy?"

Simon yelped. "You damn fool, you frightened me out of twenty years!" He hadn't heard the bartender coming behind the bar to prepare the setups for the festivity that lay ahead.

"You shouldn't talk to yourself," said the bartender, "it could become dangerous."

Simon replied with hauteur, "It's the only time I get intelligent answers!"

They heard shouting from the backstage area followed by a door slamming. The voice was muffled, but they could tell Connery was doing the shouting.

The bartender asked, "Who's he got in there with him?"

"His favorite witch. I'll give you odds it has something to do with that item in the paper this morning about Neon."

"I don't read the papers. What was the item?" Simon told him. The bartender was washing glasses. "You got any ideas about who might have killed Neon?"

"Just one, dear. Just one."

In his office, Milton Connery was pacing back and forth, spuming his wrath like a preacher in the boondocks promising hellfire and brimstone. "How the hell could you let yourself play into their hands?"

"Did I know those bastards would be there with Mae? I only went there to find out what she knew about the investigation being reopened," explained Agnes.

"Well, you sure found out, didn't you! God damn it! Ye gods!" He slammed a fist against a wall.

"That isn't going to help any, Milton. Now sit down and let's talk this over rationally. Did you hurt yourself?" He was flexing his fingers, a pained expression on his face. "Milton, Villon's got nothing on you. He's got no proof."

Connery took a bottle of scotch from a desk drawer. He produced two glasses and filled them. As he did this, he said: "He's got his suspicion and I'm *it*."

"I repeat, he's got no proof."

Connery leaned forward, a savage expression on his face, his voice an ugly rasp. "Why do you think Dvorack killed himself? Villon made him sing. He told Villon about my bribing him to ice the investigation. Dvorack was frightened into killing himself. And now Villon's going to play games with us. I know his reputation. I know all about the psychological games he plays with suspects. Damn it to hell!" He knocked back the scotch.

Agnes lit a cigarette. "Fear isn't going to help. You're a smart man, Milton. If Villon had the goods on us, he'd have picked us up yesterday. He doesn't frighten me. He doesn't frighten me one bit."

"He doesn't? So how come you're spilling ashes all over yourself?"

"Damn it!"

Connery refilled his glass and the swivel chair groaned as he sat back. "Oleandrin. It had to be something fancy like oleandrin. It couldn't have been plain old ordinary cyanide. And Amanda Harbor, for crying out loud. They're bound to find out she once worked here." His elbows rested on the desk. "Amanda Baker. Did they make them any dumber than Amanda Baker?"

"She was smart enough to find herself a safe Harbor. So help me, I didn't know she really meant to kill anybody. I thought she was content to have landed herself a meal ticket. I still remember her dropping by my place for a drink and weaseling out of me that the Witches' Brew was the place to get poison without a prescription."

"I suppose Villon knows that too?"

"When we were at Mae's together. It came up very innocently in the conversation then. Dwight will know how to handle Villon. He's tangled with the cops before."

"Who the hell are you talking about?"

"Dwight Pratt owns the Witches' Brew. He's a warlock."

"Oh, don't get started on that crap again." He was on his feet again and pacing. Worried. Frightened. There was so much at stake. It wasn't easy progressing from small-time hood to big-time club owner, although he always insisted, for income tax purposes, that he only had a small interest in the place. Bigtime blackmailer. The victims wouldn't blow their cover. It would destroy their careers. "Come on, Agnes, you got any ideas?"

"Only one. Do nothing. Sit tight. You got a big night tonight and another one tomorrow night. Go home and soak in a tub for an hour. Mae will be here with the detectives. Villon's girlfriend is Hazel Dickson, the one who buys and sells gossip. Be the affable host. Send a bottle of champagne to the table."

"Spiked with oleandrin?"

"I can't help you there. I'm fresh out. Do you hear what I'm saying?"

"I hear you."

"Bluff it out. You don't know who killed Neon. You were crazy about the kid. You were grooming him for the big time. You wish you could lay your hands on his killer. You'd mash the son of a bitch good. Why, Neon was like a son to you."

"Daughter."

Agnes smiled. "That's it, Milton. Make with the jokes. The snide remarks. Go yell at Simon LeGrand."

"Spare me. He spits and stamps his foot all the time. Sometimes I think he's going to bare fangs."

"Really? Vampire fangs?"

Milton looked at her. "Agnes, not by a long shot can I imagine Simon LeGrand as the vampire killer."

"Milton, never erase a suspicion without first making a thorough examination."

"Agnes, now it's my turn. *You* go home and soak in a hot tub." He stared at the ceiling while shaking his head with disbelief. Simon LeGrand as a killer. Just not possible.

* * *

Father Wallace Riggs was in the confessional for the eighth time that day. He wondered what it was about Hallowe'en that made certain people want to bare their souls. The voice he was listening to was a familiar one. He came to confession every day. Father Riggs was convinced the man was crazy.

"Oh, Father, forgive me, for I have sinned."

Father yawned while he forgave. "Yes, my son?"

"I am the vampire killing those Mae West impersonators."

"My son, you've been saying that for weeks."

"That's right." He could tell the man was smiling. "And you can't snitch on me to the cops because a priest can't tell what he's heard in the confessional." He paused. "Why is this place so cramped?"

"It's a standard design."

"Actually, I'm here today to give you a little treat."

"Oh, how nice."

"Sort of a preview of things to come. You know, like in the movie houses."

"I have a very busy day today."

"Now, don't get impatient. Priests aren't supposed to get impatient. Especially when they're listening to a poor soul confessing his sins."

"What's the preview?"

"Don't hurry me." He then spoke like a child taunting another one. "It's for me to know and for you to find out."

"I won't find out until you tell me."

"Exactly." Pause. "Father, you still there?"

"Of course."

"Well, here goes. First of all, I'm sorry I murdered Nedda Connolly. I really don't like killing women." Father Riggs folded his hands together and stared at them. "But I'm not sorry I murdered the homosexuals. And I'm not sorry I'm going to murder again tonight." Father Riggs remained silent. "Doesn't that shock you? Father, are you listening?"

"Yes, my son, I'm listening."

"There's going to be a lot of them out tonight for Hallowe'en."

"Who do you mean?"

"Impersonators! They'll be all over the place. They'll be at the queer clubs. The Limp Wrist. The Angry Parrot. The Purple Passion. The Tailspin. There'll be so many impersonating Mae. Oh, how my cup will runneth over!"

"Now you mustn't be a glutton. Don't make a pig of yourself."

"Oh, of course not. I can only do one every so often. Committing murder is so emotionally exhausting. But I'll be in again tomorrow to confess. I so look forward to our little chats." Pause. "Father?"

"I'm listening." He looked at his wristwatch. He hoped there was no one else waiting to confess. It got a little tiresome handing out all those Hail Marys and Stations of the Cross.

"I—I don't bore you, do I?"

"Goodness, no."

"That's good. I wouldn't want to kill you."

Cops, thought Dwight Pratt. How I loathe cops. They don't have to tell me they're cops. I can smell them a mile away. He first saw them standing on the sidewalk staring at his special Halloween window display. He did it every year. Three witches around a cauldron straight out of Shakespeare, ornately swathed in black robes decorated with sparkling paillettes. After two decades of running the Witches' Brew, the crones were getting a bit moth-eaten, a bit frayed around the edges, especially their noses and their chins. So what? It made them look that much more sinister and evil. The black cat with its back arched, its mouth contorted as if to screech. An assortment of ravens hanging by piano wire. This year there was a new touch added: a vampire. Yellow eyes, bloodred lips, sparkling fangs, dead-white face, very picturesque if not terribly frightening.

Dwight Pratt was getting impatient with Herb Villon and Jim Mallory. If they plan to come in, why don't they get a move on?

He knew why they were here. Agnes Darwin had warned him to expect them. He didn't like cops but he loved driving them around the bend with evasions and misinformation. Is it oleander you're looking for, darlings? There's a vase full of it right over there in the corner. Oleandrin, is it? You'll have to squeeze it out yourself. Don't you flat-footed darlings know it's illegal to sell poison without a prescription? Aha! They're making their move. The door opened and the bell jingled. Herb and Jim entered.

Herb thought Dwight Pratt looked like Uriah Heep, right out of *David Copperfield*. At least he looked the way Roland Young looked when he limned Uriah Heep in the movie version the previous year. Dwight Pratt was small and shriveled. He had a myopic squint despite the frameless glasses he wore. He always cocked his head to the right as though expecting a blow. One wondered if it disappointed him that none was ever delivered. Herb expected Pratt's voice to sound like an unoiled hinge, and he wasn't disappointed.

"Good afternoon, gentlemen. Welcome to my humble establishment, a delightful bit of color on drab Fairfax Avenue. If you're looking for costumes, I'm afraid I have a very limited selection. All that's left are some skeleton costumes, one warlock's outfit, and a black cat, but I don't think it would fit either one of you." Villon flashed his badge. "Good heavens! The police!" Pratt rubbed his hands together in gleeful anticipation of leading them around in circles.

Obsequious little runt, thought Villon. Jim Mallory wanted out as soon as possible. The minute he set foot into the store he'd felt a foreboding. The place was a mess. It smelled of dust and stale food. On the other hand, Villon understood the disorder. He'd experienced it before. He knew that to people like Dwight Pratt, there was order in the disorder. He was positive Pratt knew exactly where to locate any item requested. "You were recommended by Agnes Darwin."

"Dear Agnes. An exemplary witch. She's a wizard with the Tarot. We once danced a mad tango in Falcon's Lair, Rudolph Valentino's home said to be haunted by his specter. Well, my dears, we danced our little feet off for hours but Rudy didn't materialize. Fie on him, I still believe in ghosts. I've owned this store for so many years, people think *I'm* one!" He cackled. Jim Mallory considered running screaming into the street but knew Villon would look on it unfavorably. "So tell me already, what exactly is it you're looking for?"

"I trust your memory is as good as your performance."

Smart ass. I'll fix him. "Performance? You mean me? Oh, dearie me. You ain't seen nothing yet. If you hang around long enough, I go into my Bell, Book, and Candle routine. You won't sleep for days."

"Do you remember a woman named Amanda Harbor?"

"Oh, yes indeed. Foolish little snip. Poisoned her very wealthy husband but didn't get a dime. Sent up for life."

"The poison was oleandrin. Purchased here, I've been informed."

"Misinformed, dearie, misinformed. I do not sell poison. Illegal. Against the law. And I'm a very law-abiding citizen. I do sell the flower from which it is distilled, there's a vase full of them over in the corner. But there's nothing illegal about selling flowers, is there?"

Villon was looking at jars of colored liquids. "These things aren't poisonous?"

"They could be toxic if administered incorrectly. But poisonous, oh, heavens no. We witches use them in casting our spells. We also make love potions, you know, so if there' a young lady giving you a hard time and resisting your advances, give me half an hour and I'll concoct you an antidote that will guaranteedly reverse her resistance."

"If it doesn't prove fatal."

"Oh, never, never, never. You will never lay a death at my door. I am a dedicated warlock, a male witch, and tonight being Hallowe'en, a coven shall convene in my rooms above the store. A coven is thirteen witches, in case you are unfamiliar with our vocabulary. It's much like a *minyan* in the Jewish religion. A *minyan* meaning the ten men required to commence their morning and evening prayers. You can see members of the congregation running up and down Fairfax looking for conscripts for their *minyans*. Witches, contrary to old wives' tales, do not kill. We frown on homicide."

"Oleandrin kills," said Villon.

"So does cancer and heart attacks and reckless drivers and, heavens, I could go on forever."

I hope not, thought Jim Mallory. Let's get out of here. We're getting nowhere with this freak. Hollywood's a notorious breeding ground for off-the-wall eccentrics, but Mr. Pratt takes the prize. If there's a Mrs. Pratt, may God have mercy on her soul.

Villon had moved to a display case. "What are these?"

"Ah! These are my treasures!" Pratt scuttled like a crab to Villon's side. "Over here are the witch wands, a witch wouldn't be caught dead without one. You have certainly heard of the great conductor Leopold Stokowski? He bought a supply of them from me several years ago and may I say, now that he conducts his symphonies with them, their performances have vastly improved. Here we have dried spiders, dried ants, dried tail of iguana, eye of newt—a very popular item—snuff, and stale corn flakes for very special brews. Some of my ladies and gentlemen are very ingenious in the brews they concoct. Foul smelling and foul tasting, but if you're brave enough to take the plunge, very effective."

Villon was kneeling for a better look at some items on the bottom shelf of the display case. "Aren't those fangs?"

"Good heavens but you're perceptive." He opened the display case and brought forth the tray of fangs. Jim Mallory, his curiosity piqued, joined them for a closer look. "See?" He had two fangs in the palm of his hands. "Sold a good lot of these this week. Those vampire murders have proven somewhat inspirational. There are going to be quite a number of vampires flitting about out there tonight." He placed the fangs, one on a tooth, on either side of his mouth, his display of yellowed teeth filling Mallory with disgust. "There. A little clumsy to handle but practice makes perfect and in no time you can sink them into someone's throat with devil-may-care alacrity!" His smile was as repulsive as he was. "Ouch! Oh, dear, I've bitten my lips. Oh, dearie me no, I'd never be comfortable as a vampire." He removed the fangs and unsanitarily placed them back among the others. "What have you found there? Mr. Detective, what's that item you're palming? Oh, the bat ring. Good heavens, I forgot I had another one."

In the palm of his hand, Villon held a piece of jewelry that made his heart leap. His eyes locked with Mallory's and Jim was equally elated. The ring was shaped like a bat's head with two protruding fangs.

"Careful, dearie," cautioned Mr. Pratt. "Those fangs can cause a deadly puncture."

Villon asked, "How much?"

"For you, dearie? Since you haven't hassled me, fifty dollars. And that's a bargain!"

"I'll take it." Pratt took the ring to place in a box while Villon selected two twenties and a ten from his wallet.

As Pratt wrapped the box into a neat little package, he prattled away breezily. "This ring's a collector's item. It had a twin but I sold that many months ago to a young man."

Villon felt a tingle, the kind that told him he was getting a much needed lead. "Do you remember his name?"

"Oh, yes. A dear little thing. He's dead. Murdered. There was something about him in this morning's paper. Neon Light. Not his real name, of course. He bought the ring as a birthday present for a relative. His brother, I think he said. Oh, my dears! Talk about coincidence! It was Agnes Darwin who sent him here! She is so generous with her recommendations. She should be in real estate. Here you are, all nicely wrapped. And thank you for the fifty. What lovely crisp new bills! Did you also want some oleanders? They're only five dollars a dozen."

"No, thank you," Villon said as he pocketed the small box, "I'm very happy with the ring." And with the little tidbits of information that came gushing out of your foul little mouth, dearie.

"Do come back again. I love it when someone's as appreciative of my little establishment as you are." He asked Mallory,

"Oh, dearie, aren't you feeling well? You have such a look of disgust on your face."

Mallory said nothing and fled outside with Villon in his wake. Villon asked, "Aren't you feeling well, dearie? I'm feeling just great. This ring. Its twin. Whoever owns that twin is our killer. Now to track down Neon's brother."

"Herb, that little rodent Pratt could have been feeding us a line. Neon could have bought the ring as a gift for someone else, like maybe Milton Connery."

"Jim, my money's on the brother. I want to get my hands on that file. I want to track down Neon's adoptive parents, the Williamsons. They just might give us a lead as to the brother's whereabouts." A thought struck him as they walked to their unmarked police car. "Who buried Neon? Who claimed his body?"

"Probably the Williamsons."

"Better still, maybe the brother. Let's go back to precinct pronto. I want that file, and I want you to find out from the morgue what mortuary handled Neon's funeral and who arranged it. I'm feeling real good, Jimmy boy, real real good!"

"You're lookin' real good, Bev. Real good. In fact, you're lookin' so real good, I'm beginnin' to wonder which one of us is which. I'm wearin' black tonight, so I'd like you to wear white. That way we can tell each other apart. Whaddya think of my bodyguards?" Her eyes twinkled. One of the few things Mae West and her sister had in common besides their uncanny resemblance to each other was their taste in body builders.

"I wish you didn't need them."

"Amen," said Desdemona, who had brought in the tea cart with refreshments to sustain the sisters until dinner at the Tailspin.

"Now, listen you two, and you can pass it on to Goneril, I don't want any crepe hangin' around here any more. Things are black enough as they are and it's infectin' my performance in the pitcher. Now seriously, Bev, whoever this killer is, he ain't got much discrimination. If you're goin' around dressed like me and talkin' like me, you're a marked woman. So you gotta be careful. Until they catch this nut case, you're stickin' close to me, attached at the hip. I can't send Timony out to round up another team of bodyguards. The traffic around here is heavy enough as it is. To be perfectly frank, much as I'm glad to see you, I wish you had stayed back East."

"To tell you the truth, Mae, I wish that too. But I ain't cancelin' my bookin', it's unprofessional."

Mae threw a heaven-help-me look at the ceiling. "Boy, where were you when they were handin' out the brains? Desdemona, what are you hangin' around for? We can help ourselves. Thank God you and your sister ain't goin' to the Tailspin dressed up like me."

"I don't think he'd kill a black Mae West, do you?" Desdemona eyes were about to pop.

"He don't give a damn about black or white or pink, it's the thought that counts. Now beat it, you're makin' me nervous."

Desdemona hurried back to the kitchen. Jim Timony had gone to his apartment nearby to change his clothes. Seymour Steel Cheeks was in the garage applying wax to the Rolls-Royce. Mae was preparing to soak in the bathtub for a while and advised Beverly to do the same.

"Mae, haven't you a clue as to why this maniac is after you?" Beverly was stirring honey into her tea, said to be good for the complexion.

"As a matter of fact I do. I think it has something to do with Neon and his brother. You see, Brother was against Neon's becoming a female impersonator. In fact, Neon said he got pretty violent about it. Well, I'm the one that encouraged Neon. So Neon gets murdered, and this I think is what may have sent his brother around the bend. I think he figures if he hadn't gone into the impersonation business, he wouldn't have gotten in with the kind of people that led him to get murdered. And he's right. I shoulda stuck out of it. I should have left the kid alone. But I was a sucker for that sweet face of his and the way he worshiped me. And he did, Bev, the kid absolutely worshiped me."

"It's not your fault he took the wrong path, Mae."

"Well, I didn't have no control over Milton Connery throwin' stardust in the kid's eyes. I think it was learnin' he didn't have long to live that warped Neon's mind. He made a bad move and the poor little bastard paid for it."

"Well, it wasn't your fault, Sis!"

"Sure it wasn't my fault," stormed Mae, "so go find that nutty brother of his and convince *him*. Anyway, there's nothin' to be done about it tonight. Now, listen Bev, go easy on your date. He's a nice guy, and he's a little shy. None of that squeezin' his thigh under the table."

"I don't do that any more!" Beverly seethed with indignation.

"Oh, no? So what do you squeeze?"

"I don't squeeze nothin'!" She refilled her cup. "By the way, Mae, what's with the Indian?"

"You lay off him. I ain't ready to dump him. I've handed you enough of my discarded lovers in the past, but I ain't ready to discard this one. I got too much on my mind what with the vampire and my pitcher, and I ain't got the time right now to audition a replacement." She thought for a moment. "Maybe I'll be through with him come Thanksgivin' and then you'll have somethin' to be thankful for, but until then, lay off or I'll belt you one. I'm gonna take my bath." When she reached her bedroom, she paused in the entrance. "We're gonna drive them nuts when they see us together!"

FOURTEEN

NEON'S FILE WAS ON THE DESK when Villon and Mallory returned to the office. Villon said, "God is looking kindly on us today. I must have done a good deed without realizing it." He sat and eagerly opened the folder. He didn't expect to find much and he wasn't disappointed. "For a slob, Felix kept a meticulous file. Look at this garbage." He mumbled as his eyes scanned the few pages. "Michael Williamson a.k.a. Neon Light . . ." Mumble mumble mumble. ". . . found in Griffith Park . . . skull crushed . . ." Mumble mumble mumble. 'Interrogated Simon LeGrand . . . manager at Tailspin Club where deceased had been appearing . . ." Mumble mumble mumble, while Mallory contemplated the window behind Villon. "Interrogated Milton Connery . . . distraught . . . such a great performer . . . such a nice boy . . . et cetera et cetera et cetera . . . No feasible leads . . . dead end . . . body claimed by Nicholas and Maria Williamson . . ." Villon looked up. "There's an address here for them. Cynthia Avenue. That's between Sunset and Santa Monica, on the border of Beverly Hills. No need to bother with a mortuary. Let's go."

Twenty minutes later they stood in front of a burned-out house on Cynthia Avenue. "You sure this is the address?" Mallory asked Villon.

148

"I'm sure. Damn it." He crossed to the house, which was set some fifty feet back from the sidewalk. All that remained was a charred shell.

"Nick and Maria were killed." It was a woman who spoke in a cultured voice and introduced herself as Helen Maynard. Villon recognized her face. She'd been a leading lady in several popular westerns. She was pleased he recognized her, she'd been out of films for years and sounded as though she had no regrets. "Nicholas and Maria did stunt work. Maria used to double for me. I'm terrified of horses. Were you friends of theirs?" Villon showed her his badge and explained he and hsi associate were investigating Neon's murder and the murders of the vampire killer's victims. She grimaced. "Nasty business."

Villon indicated the charred remains of the house. "How long ago did this happen?"

"About a week after Mickey's funeral. I mean Neon, I suppose. I hated that name."

"Do you know what caused the fire?"

"It was an explosion of some kind. I live across the street in the blue bungalow. The explosion awakened me. It was around three in the morning. The flames engulfed the house in what seemed like just a matter of a few minutes. It was horrible. I phoned for help. By the time the fire engines got here, it was too late."

"The Williamsons were trapped?"

"It was horrible. They must have died instantly, or at least for their sake I hope so." She paused and then continued with difficulty. "There wasn't a sound from them."

"Were you told what caused the explosion?"

"They had some propane stored in the basement. It was supposed that it was spontaneous combustion." She looked Villon straight in the eye. "I have a propensity toward melodramatics. My suspicion is that it was arson. That the Williamsons were murdered. They had their suspicions as to who murdered Neon, and they made loud protests about the bungling police investigation. The man in charge was named Dvorack. You know, the one written up in the papers. The suicide. You probably knew him."

"We knew him."

"Nicholas and Maria loathed him. He told them to quit pestering him at the station house. They were considering hiring a private eye of their own, and told him so."

"That was a tragic mistake," said Villon.

"So I'm right. They were murdered. I think they were dead before the fire was set."

"Lady, you've got a detective's mind." He added quickly, "An honest detective's mind."

"We'll never know how they were killed. Maria's sister had the remains cremated. At least, she hoped it was their remains. The fire did quite a nasty number on them. I'm looking for someplace else to live. Seeing this devastation every day is nerve-wracking."

"Did you know Neon's brother?"

"I knew he had one but I never set eyes on him. I don't think he ever came to the house to see Neon. I think Maria told me they met in coffeeshops or the brother took him for a drive. He disapproved of Neon's drag act and disapproved of the Williamsons for permitting it. But Neon somehow became friendly with Mae West, he was so crazy about her, and she convinced Neon to pursue his career. Did you ever see him?" Neither of them had. "He was a natural. An uncanny performer. He gave me goose pimples, his impersonations were that accurate. Too bad they were never filmed."

"The Williamsons ever tell you who they suspected murdered Neon? His brother perhaps?"

"Never his brother. He was devoted to Neon. Nicholas and Maria think Neon was murdered because he knew too much about a shady operation backstage at the Tailspin." She favored them with a cynical smile. "From the looks on your faces, I've struck oil."

"Did they know he was incurably ill?"

She was genuinely shocked. "Oh, no! How awful. I'm sure they didn't know. They would have told me. Poor guy." She shrugged. "I guess somebody up there wasn't crazy about him." Her face hardened. "I hope you find the bastard soon. I'd like to pay him a visit when he's behind bars and spit in his face."

A child's voice interrupted them. "Why, hello there folks." In a dreadful imitation of Mae West. "How'd ya like t' come up'n see me sometime?" Then with hands on hips, a string purse dangling from her left wrist, she whined, "Trick or treat?"

Villon stared at her with revulsion. Mallory and Helen Maynard were obviously equally repulsed. The child was about eight or nine years old. Her lips and cheeks were heavily rouged. Her eyelids were a sickening shade of blue. Her eyelashes were heavy with mascara. Her eyebrows had been tweezed into thin lines. She wore a filthy old blond wig. Her dress was a makeshift imitation of a gown of the turn of the century and her high-heeled shoes, probably her mother's, looked as though they could accommodate another pair of feet. The child looked like a perverted midget.

"Well," she insisted obnoxiously, "trick or treat?"

Mallory fished in his pocket and found a coin, which he gave her. It was a five-cent piece. "Thanks, mister," she said as she tucked it into her string purse. "I hope it doesn't break you," she added nastily.

As they watched her clip-clop away, swinging her hips exaggeratedly from side to side, Mallory said loud enough for Villon and Helen Maynard to hear him, "Oh, Mr. Vampire Killer, come quick, come quick to Cynthia Street." The three shared a much-needed laugh.

"Morris! You're leaving me home alone again?" Goldie Rothfeld was in the kitchen kneading dough for a coffee cake.

The rabbi stood in front of a mirror that hung from a hook in the wall fixing his tie. "Condolence calls, Goldie, condolence calls, you forgot?"

"I try to forget because there are so many people dying these days. Is it so necessary? You keep telling me it's because God is lonely and wants company. Why does he choose so much company from Hollywood?"

"Because He's a name dropper probably. How should I know!"

"Be careful out there, Morris. There's a murderer on the loose."

"I'm not a Mae West impersonator. I'm safe."

"But you sing with a high falsetto."

He was losing patience. "I'm not going to sing on the street. And besides, I'm a big boy with muscles and a solid punch. I'm not afraid of anything and don't you be. Look at Miss West. She's really got something to be frightened about, but is she frightened? Not her. The rock of Gibralter with curves. And, oi, what curves. Don't be jealous, Goldie. I only look. I never touch."

She put the batter aside and wiped her hands with a dish towel. "Morris." It was her I-mean-business tone of voice.

He moved away from the mirror. "I'm looking at you. What?"

"What's bothering you?"

"Nothing's bothering me."

"The way you said that I'm more positive something's bothering you."

"Stop nagging."

"I'm not nagging, I'm worried."

"Stop worrying."

"I'll stop worrying when you tell me what's bothering you."

He knew when he was beaten. "I'm worried about Miss West."

"Why? Because if she dies you'll lose a generous patron?"

"Goldie," he said sharply, "that's a terrible thing to say!"

"Why is the truth always so terrible?" Her shoulders were raised and her hands were outstretched. "When I took my marriage vows did I suspect I was also taking an oath of poverty?"

"We're not so bad off."

"We're not so good off either."

He raised his voice. "When you married me you knew rabbis never become wealthy!"

"I didn't know we'd leave Richmond Hill in New York to come to this godforsaken hole."

"Don't say that in a synagogue! It's a sin against God!"

"He takes good care of Himself! He's doing just fine! We aren't! Let's go back to New York where you have a chance with your gorgeous voice. You were doing all right playing the Catskills when I met you. Here you don't play nothing."

"My responsibility is to my congregation right here. Now that's enough, Goldie."

"There's never enough, Morris!"

"Goldie, when you start getting me upset I feel like going outside and murdering somebody!"

She stared at him. "How come not me?"

"Because, God forgive me, I love you too much. Don't wait up for me. I'll be late."

"Why?"

The Tailspin Club sounded like a dozen chicken coops invaded by a dozen foxes. Here cacophony attained a pantheon as a fine art. While the noise was eardrum-shattering, even with the counterpoint of a six-piece orchestra dressed in skeleton suits and playing "The Darktown Strutter's Ball," the assemblage in variegated plumage were a feast for the eyes. It was almost impossible to tell the men from the women. Freelance photographers pushed their way through the dance floor whenever they spotted a celebrity either at a table or making an entrance. Money would later exchange hands in return for the negatives. Little Bo-Peep danced with Little Miss Muffet, both baritones. They bumped into two people who announced they were Doctor Jekyll and Mr. Hide. Mr. Hyde said to them, "You'll have to excuse Doctor Jekyll. He's not himself." An Arabian sheik eating a pastrami sandwich told them, "I'm the Deli Lama." Frankenstein's monster and his bride were at the bar and, at this early hour, already three sheets to the wind. The bartender explained to Alice in Wonderland, who had hairy legs, hairy arms, and held on for dear life to the Mad Hatter who was hitting people with his purse, "They were married yesterday. They're both lushes. It was a shotglass wedding."

Agnes Darwin was a striking and exotic Morgan LeFay, straight out of *A Connecticut Yankee in King Arthur's Court*. There were so many witch costumes in the room, she was glad she had decided to forgo hers. Milton Connery, wearing a tuxedo, was talking to Simon LeGrand, who had wriggling toy snakes in his wig, a rather interesting looking Medusa. Agnes wished she could read lips. Milton was still agitated and Simon was his usual unruffled self.

The three bartenders were skillfully filling demanding orders while bantering with the patrons and fielding sexual innuendos and sexual propositions.

The Mae West impersonators were beginning to arrive. It was almost nine o'clock and the room was atip awaiting the entrance of the real thing. Mussolini and Haile Selassie arrived arm in arm wearing ballet slippers and tutus and proceeded to do an adagio that probably had the great Russian choreographer Petipas spinning in his grave. Romeo and Juliet were doing lewd things in the entrance to the hallway leading to the bathrooms. Simon LeGrand hurried to them and cautioned them to behave themselves.

Honk!

Simon LeGrand crossed himself as Goneril came tearing into the club as Harpo Marx trailed by Desdemona as Marlene Dietrich. They headed straight for the bar and ordered brandy Alexanders. "Two alcoholic malted milks coming right up," shouted Jason, the bartender who had startled Simon LeGrand earlier that day when he was pasting tinsel to the bar mirror. Through the reflections in the mirror Desdemona and Goneril saw a Mae West duplicate approaching them with arms outstretched. She was much too bulky to be the real thing. Goneril said to Desdemona, "God in heaven, it's Billie Doux!" The three squealed and hugged each other, the production secretary on Mae's film commandeering a bottle of beer from Jason.

"Say, listen," she said to the black ladies, "how can you tell which of these guys are the real thing?"

Goneril advised her, "Honey, on Hallowe'en you don't even try. Not in this town."

"I'm awful tired of being all alone when I lower my lamp," said Billie Doux and then took a healthy swig of her beer.

Said Goneril, "There are an awful lot of Miss West imitators here tonight. Somehow I'm feeling a little uneasy."

"Honeybunch, don't give it a second thought," pooh-pooh'd Billie Doux. "Take a look at this room. It's mob rule. If any vampire tried to put the bite on anyone tonight he'd be stampeded and strung up, so relax. This is vampire's night off."

Milton Connery said to Agnes Darwin, "You're not working the room."

"I can't budge. I've been trying to get to the bar for the past fifteen minutes, but a surge of unnatural humanity keeps driving me back."

"Come on," he said as he grabbed her hand and pushed their way to the bar.

Agnes managed a glance at her wristwatch. Almost nine o'clock. Time for Mae to arrive with her party. Then the probability of matching wits with Herb Villon. They passed a table populated with several Hollywood players who were brave enough not to camouflage their homosexuality and as a result cornered the market in films as butlers, salesmen, perpetually flustered hotel clerks, and maître d's and, in the case of comedian Edward Everett Horton, just about every leading man's best friend and advisor. He was discussing an ingenue rapidly gaining a reputation for easy virtue, with his lover, actor Gavin Gordon, who in 1930 had been Greta Garbo's leading man in *Romance* and then rapidly descended to bit parts. Horton told him, "She claims she didn't lose her virginity, she just misplaced it."

"Now really, Eddie," said Franklin Pangborn, another table companion familiar to moviegoers for his snappy way with a line of dialogue. "I know her extremely well. She's good to the navy but rotten to the corps. God, will you look at all the Mae Wests!"

"What?" exclaimed Horton. "No vampires?"

"I stood next to one in the men's room," simpered Pangborn. "But I couldn't interest him in a fang bang."

"Frankie and Johnnie were lovers . . ."

The orchestra managed to be heard above the din. Simon LeGrand signaled an electrician who lowered the overhead lights and switched on a huge spotlight, centering it on Mae West. Mae stood at the top of the stairs dressed in a beaded black gown, black feathers in her hair, a wealth of diamonds on her fingers and wrists, a diamond choker around her neck, and a black feathered stole draped around her neck. She held Jim Timony's arm and rewarded the room with a lavish smile when it erupted with deafening applause, shrieks, whistles, and foot stomping. Their goddess had arrived and the acolytes wanted her to know how sincerely they loved her. Then the clamor heightened as Beverly West stepped into the spotlight with Mae and Timony. She was in a sequined white dress, her fingers and wrists festooned with fake diamonds. In her hair she wore an arrangement of multicolored ribbons. Most of the merrymakers were hard put to tell which Mae West was the real Mae West. Mae and Timony ascended slowly, Beverly behind them with her arm through Jim Mallory's. Herb Villon followed with Hazel Dickson dressed in a green velvet evening gown with brown accessories, which made her look like the prima donna of a third-rate traveling opera company. Behind them were the three bodyguards who soon were the cynosures of a very specialized group of admirers. Simon LeGrand crossed the dance floor to greet Mae and led her and her party to the table reserved for them near the orchestra. Simon then signaled the electrician and once again the overhead lights glistened. Simon wasn't taking any chances with dimmed lighting, not in this room and not with this crowd, whom he referred to as exponents of grope therapy.

While several waiters took their orders and set about filling them, Timony asked Mae why she was frowning. "It's all these here imitators of me. Look at them. All shapes and sizes. And I seen a couple of vampires. I'm gettin' uneasy." She snapped her fingers at a waiter. "Say, listen, tall, dark, and handsome." He was short, pale, and homely but preferred Mae's description. "I'd like to talk to the manager of this jernt."

"You mean Simon LeGrand or Mr. Connery, who's over at the bar with Miss Darwin?"

"Oh, yeah. I see them." Her eyes returned to the waiter. "Whichever is most available. I'll leave the cherce up to you, cutie."

Simon LeGrand chose the moment to come to the table followed by two waiters bearing several bottles of champagne. He said to Mae, "Compliments of the management."

She smiled and said, "I'm sure there's more than champagne that needs coolin' tonight." The waiters were slowly twirling the bottles in their coolers. She said to Simon, "Now which management are you?"

He introduced himself. "Is there something I can do for you?"

"As a matter of fact there is." She explained what she wanted and he offered her his arm. She took it and he guided her up the three steps that led to the bandstand. The orchestra leader, a natural toady, rewarded her with his best sycophantic smile, grabbed her hand, and kissed it while Mae murmured, "Stop slobberin'." Simon heard her and guffawed. "Now, Mr. Orchestra Leader," said Mae, wishing she had something with which to dry her hand, "I want to say a few words to the crowd. So if you'll give me a fanfare and a couple of drum rolls, you'll be wallowin' in my gratitude."

"Your wish is my command," the orchestra leader said in a voice that made her skin crawl. In a few seconds, there was a fanfare and a drum roll and Simon signaled for a spotlight on Mae. Hazel Dickson, never without a small pad of paper, was scribbling away, having spotted Edward Everett Horton and his party. Louella Parson would certainly go for this item.

The room erupted as they saw Mae take her position at the microphone in the baby pink spotlight. She stood with hands on hips, sparkling in the spotlight, an insinuating smile on her face, the one that promised everything but delivered nothing, and waited for the commotion to die down.

"In case you're wonderin', I'm the real thing." Big laugh. She smiled. "I'm up here now because I think it's important I get a little serious for a couple of minutes, then you can go back to misbehavin'." Good laugh. "I was young myself once, but I didn't realize it at the time." Applause and big laugh. "I hate to remind you but I think it's necessary because I see so many of my imitators are here tonight. You all look great and I'm very flattered, because as any broad who wears fake jewelry can tell you, imitation is the sincerest form of flattery." Beverly West managed to keep her composure with a sweet smile on her face. Mae continued in a serious vein. "But I don't have to tell you, there's a dangerous killer on the loose. He's killed four of my imitators to date, and he's out to kill more. He's supposed to be a vampire, but my friend Herb Villon, who's here with me tonight, tells me he's just plain old flesh and blood, and a certifiable maniac. If he's here tonight"—the guests began soberly sizing other guests up as she continued with a sly smile—"if I've hurt his feelings, forgive me, I've got no regrets. I'd rather be hurtin' his feelin's than have him hurtin' mine. So, listen all of you other Mae Wests out there, be careful, remember there's safety in numbers, and I don't mean telephone numbers." Nice laugh. "Travel around the place in twos and threes. Don't even go to the terlet alone. And if for some reason you need some fresh air, don't go outside alone. Now, I'd like you to meet my sister Beverly who's openin' *her* Mae West act here tomorrow night. It's her first engagement on the West Coast, so I want you to give her a real big Hollywood welcome." Mae signaled for the spotlight to move to Beverly and, while it did, she thanked the boys in the orchestra, dodged the leader who was out to commandeer her hand again, and gave her hand to Simon, who led her back to the table. Beverly glowed as the crowd gave her an ovation and finally sat. Mallory smiled and then grunted as Beverly squeezed his thigh under the table.

Villon said to Mae, "Thanks for not giving it away."

"Givin' what away?"

"The vampire ring."

"You nuts or somethin'? Tell them about the ring and put the killer's guard up? No way. Oh, for cryin' out loud. Will you look at Goneril and Desdemona! What are those drinks they're beltin'?"

Timony said, "From here they look like brandy Alexanders."

"There's gonna be a lot of Bromo Seltzer fizzin' around the apartment tomorrow." She said to the bodyguards, "How you boys doin'?"

Salvatore Puccini said, "I've had an awful lot of pieces of paper with names and phone numbers slipped into my pockets."

"Well, just be careful they don't slip anything out of your pockets. Especially your pants pockets. Say, Selma . . ."

"Yes, ma'am?"

"Do me a favor. Go to the bar and see how Desdemona and Goneril are holdin' up. They seem to be doin' an awful lot of drinkin'."

"That would be my pleasure, Miss West," he said, flashing his two rows of perfect ivories.

Mae smiled back. "I thought you'd like that. Just remember, they're God-fearin' ladies. Well, well, well. What do I see approachin'?"

Three young men dressed in biblical garb came to the table and bowed in unison.

Mae said to the others, "Don't you recognize them? Didn't any of you ever read the Bible? These three are Caspar, Melchior, and Balthazar. They're the Maggies, the three wise men who saw a star that led them to Bethlehem. Well, here they are again, seein' a different kind of star. Boys, if they're givin' prizes tonight, you deserve one." They giggled and asked for her autograph. She signed their programs graciously. After they left, she said to Herb Villon, "Agnes and Connery aren't exactly breakin' their necks to join us."

"Don't worry, Mae. The night is young."

"Yeah, but from the looks of the two of them at the bar, they're aging rapidly."

FIFTEEN

THE TAILSPIN'S GARDEN WAS ALMOST DESERTED. Some stars and a crescent moon provided inadequate lighting. The tables and chairs were unoccupied. Simon LeGrand and Milton Connery had conferred about perhaps stringing Japanese lanterns and fairy lights and setting up a bar, but then decided there was not enough of a work force to police both the garden and the club interior. They weren't concerned with the thought of some revelers using the dark garden for some censorable activities. They weren't policemen and they weren't censors. Halloween night in Hollywood meant "Anything goes." And anything was going. Regardless of the fact the night was still young, there was some activity under way that would have stopped the heart of anybody's Aunt Hattie in Peoria. But this wasn't Peoria. This was Hollywood, Sodom by the Sea, condemned weekly from certain pulpits.

Billie Doux was getting an education that had no price on it. She had gone out into the garden for some fresh air and a cigarette while Simon LeGrand was leading Mae West up the stairs to the band stand. She was poking around in her small handbag for a cigarette while Mae was exhorting her audience to practice caution. She found a cigarette and put it in her mouth while she felt around for matches. The flame of a ciga-

161

rette lighter startled her. She looked up at a masked man dressed as the caped crusader. Well, of all things, Superman wearing a blue mask dotted with red spangles was lighting her cigarette.

"Thank you, Mr. Superman," she drawled à la Mae West. Having been working with her for the past three weeks, Billie had perfected a fairly accurate impersonation of the star.

She heard his hoarse voice cautioning her "You shouldn't be out here alone."

"But I'm not alone. You're here, handsome." She hoped he was. The mask obscured his face. The cape obscured his body. "Can I offer you a cigarette?"

"No, thank you. I noticed you talking to those raucous black women at the bar."

"They ain't raucous. They work for me. One's my cook, one's my maid. Where I go, they go."

"Do you imitate Miss West professionally?"

Billie was gay, feeling no pain. "Why, I'm an original. When they made me, they threw the mold away." Billie gasped. She was feeling pain. Something had punctured her throat. She was too stunned to scream, yet her mouth was open and the cigarette fell to the ground. The knife thrust into her heart stunned her. She stumbled backward, thoroughly astonished. She wanted to say, "Hey! Lay off! I'm only kidding!" But her mouth was filled with blood erupting from her insides, leaving no room for words to form. Her knees were sagging. Her arms flailed about feebly. Superman watched her pitch forward. He wiped the fangs with the hem of her costume. He pocketed the bat's head ring and glided away from the dead woman. He slipped back into the club unnoticed. It wasn't a club any longer, it was the Tower of Babel. Everywhere he looked he was confronted with bedlam. The orchestra was belting out "The Music Goes Round," the big novelty hit of the year with its deafening lyric "Yo ho ho ho ho ho and it comes out here." It was coming out anywhere and everywhere.

Simon LeGrand wiped perspiration from his face with a napkin and wished he could get drunk. He saw Beverly West dancing with Jim Mallory, who had a silly grin on his face while her mouth moved as though it were well oiled for perpetual movement, and it moved perpetually. He dwelled on her opening the next night. There was a larger number of table reservations then Milton Connery had the right to expect. Such was the power of the name West, be it Mae or Beverly. It looked as though lucky Beverly would prove a profit in reflected glory. Mae didn't seem to mind her sister trading in on her celebrity. Why should she? She was secure. She had it made. Her fame would go on forever and would probably linger a long time after her death. Mae could afford to offer a small piece of the limelight to her less fortunate sibling. Simon thought Milton Connery was ill advised booking Beverly without an audition. On the other hand, a friend whose taste he trusted had traveled from Manhattan to Coney Island in Brooklyn to catch Beverly's act at a Gay Nineties' saloon. His report to Simon was favorable.

Simon was mesmerized by Mae's table. He hadn't noticed Milton Connery and Agnes Darwin join the party. Connery was seated next to Beverly's vacant chair. There was much to discuss with her. How many numbers would she do? How long was her act? Pray God less than thirty minutes. Nobody in Hollywood had much of an attention span, not even if the headliner was an Al Jolson or a Bing Crosby. What about her orchestrations? The Tailspin's band was a small one. Here it is, that's all there is. How much rehearsal does she need or want? Pray God again they rehearse after one o'clock. He needed sleep tonight. He need a lot of sleep. Connery had been riding him for the past two days. Nothing pleased him. He was jittery. He was on edge. Something's frightening him. Agnes is as cool as a cucumber, although she's chain smoking. Beverly and Jim Mallory were back at the table. He hadn't seen Seymour Steel Cheeks join the table. Where'd he been all this time? Probably had trouble finding a parking space. Probably parked the car blocks away. Simon wondered if Mae West knew her Indian lover dropped into the Tailspin on his own on occasion to barter his body for trade. It looks like Connery is turning on that phony charm of his with Beverly. That Hazel Dickson doesn't stop scribbling in her notebook. Nobody's eating their club sandwiches. I don't blame them. I doubt if I'll ever find the appetite I lost an hour ago. Mae's manager is none too happy. She's too busy talking to the detective. Oh, my, my, my! Where did Superman come from? That mad mask, that crazy cape. He can't fool me. He's acting as though he's fascinated by the nutty goings-on on the dance floor. He's eavesdropping. He's listening to every word at Mae West's table. So what? No skin off my nose. I'm dying for a drink.

Villon was saying to Milton Connery "You read about Felix Dvorack's suicide?"

"What's so special about Felix Dvorack?" A waiter refilled his champagne glass.

"Don't tell me you've forgotten him so soon? He was the detective on Neon Light's murder."

Mae was fascinated by the knowing look on Jim Mallory's face. He was recognizing what Villon was up to. The special technique she'd heard about that he used when subtly setting up an entrapment. Mae waved the waiter away before he could refill her glass. She'd had two, which was one more than usual, and Beverly was drinking too much.

Connery was thinking—a very good job of acting, thought Mae. "Dvorack, Dvorack, oh, yes. Slightly uncouth as I recall."

"And now slightly dead," said Villon. "I still don't know if suicide is a work of courage or cowardice."

"Any idea why he killed himself?" Connery felt Agnes's eyes on him and darted her a quick look that imparted nothing.

"Oh, yes. I've got the inside dope. We were having a serious conversation a few minutes before he stuck the pistol in his mouth and pulled the trigger."

"Oh, please!" exclaimed Beverly as she shuddered and pushed her sandwich aside.

Villon ignored her and continued addressing Connery. "Dvorack was on the take. He took a bribe for hiding Neon Light's dossier in the station house basement. The deal included Dvorack dropping the investigation altogether. Too bad about Felix, he was just months away from retirement and his monthly pension. He might have gotten away with it if the vampire killer hadn't gone on his rampage. It was Mae who connected Neon's death to the impersonator murders."

Mae said to Connery, "You haven't forgotten how close Neon and me was. Practically Siamese twins for a while there."

Connery said to the others, "I always said Mae was a very clever woman."

"So does Mae," said Beverly. Mae shot her a look that was almost fatal. Beverly decided to renew interest in the sandwich she had so recently and cruelly rejected.

Connery said, "I still can't figure out why anyone would want to murder Neon. He was harmless."

Villon explained, "Not to his killer he wasn't. It turns out Neon was something of a split personality. On the surface, all sweetness and light and a good entertainer. Under the surface, a bit of a nasty blackmailer. Which is why he was poisoned."

"Poisoned?" Agnes had spoken up. "His skull was crushed."

"Oh, that was after he was dead," said Villon. "The skull was crushed in Griffith Park when the body was dumped there. Neon was poisoned elsewhere." He looked around, hoping the bedlam wouldn't permanently impair his hearing. There was so much he was planning to listen to. "Neon could have been killed here, here in the club."

Connery betrayed nothing. Mae would later admit to Villon that much as she loathed the man, she had to admire Connery's composure under fire. "Neon's body, you read, was exhumed and autopsied. He was killed by a poison named oleandrin. Agnes can tell you all about oleandrin." Agnes exhaled a smoke ring that flew past Villon's ear. Lucky for Villon, thought Mae, it ain't a bullet. "Very esoteric poison. Doesn't surface too often. The last time my coroner heard about it was when Amanda Harbor poisoned her husband. She met him when she was a hatcheck girl. Name of Amanda Baker. I have an idea she might have worked here once."

"Come to think of it, I think she did. Pretty but dumb."

Villon now zeroed in on Agnes. "By the way, Agnes, thanks for sending me to Dwight Pratt. He was very interesting, wasn't he, Jim?"

Timony looked startled but soon realized Villon meant Jim Mallory. Mallory said, "Very interesting. He made me sick to my stomach."

"Connery, you met Neon's adoptive parents, didn't you?" Villon had everyone's attention. Hazel had stopped scribbling and hung on his every word. She was hearing information that had not appeared in the newspapers. There was a dollar sign on every word Villon spoke. Hazel was contemplating a killing, a bloodless killing.

Milton Connery, thought Mae, is now very uncomfortable. He's loosening his tie and collar. And what's with Superman? He seems to be frozen in time and space. What's going on behind that campy mask?

"Yes. The Williamsons came to some of his performances. They loved Neon. They were very proud of him."

"My associate and I," said Villon, "looked the Williamsons up this afternoon. Their house was a burned-out shell." Mae had heard this on the drive from her apartment to the club. Villon had sent Mallory to escort Hazel while he met with Mae to tell her about the day's discoveries. "We met a friend of theirs who told us there was an explosion that ripped the house apart. The Williamsons were trapped by fire. The friend suspects they'd already been murdered before the explosion, which was probably a coverup."

"This is all news to me," said Connery. "I don't remember anything in the papers about it."

"It happened about a week after Neon's funeral. Their friend told us that Nicholas Williamson was planning on hiring a private eye to track down Neon's murderer, he was so disgusted with Dvorack's ineptitude. Now, Dvorack was anything but inept. He wasn't very likable, but he was certainly very capable. Until he deliberately botched the investigation. It was obvious he'd been paid off. And it's obvious the Williamsons

166

were murdered because they wanted to keep the investigation alive, even if it meant spending their own money."

Connery cleared his throat, sipped some champagne, and said, "Neon had a brother. What about *him*? He's some kind of religious nut. He said Neon in drag was a sin against God. Neon told me all this. The son of a bitch was giving Neon a hard time." Superman was staring at Connery.

"That's not who killed Neon," said Villon, nailing each word to Connery's ear. "Neon was killed because he was threatening blackmail. Threatening to name names in a racket that linked orgies to hidden cameras and photograph negatives for sale to the highest bidder, that of course being the subject of the photograph."

Mae interrupted. As far as she was concerned, she'd been silent too long. "Somebody once tried to blackmail me with some incriminatin' snapshots. I liked them so much, I bought them to illustrate a book I was plannin' to write about sex. Frankly, I didn't realize I knew so many positions." Villon could tell she was putting them on.

Villon was back at Connery. "There's all sorts of rumors that your club is a hotbed of orgies, Connery."

Connery laughed and waved a hand in the direction of the dance floor and the freelance photographers who were having a field day. Bulbs flashed, thighs flashed, a Mae West impersonator was doing a shimmy on the bar and then Mae's eyes popped as Desdemona climbed onto the bar and stole the imitator's limelight with a spirited cancan. Connery said, "There's your orgy and there's your photographers, and you can't tell me it's illegal."

"This isn't an orgy, this is a carnival," said Villon. "The real stuff goes on elsewhere. Neon knew because I suspect he participated for a fee." He leaned forward. "Neon was desperate. He was dying."

Connery exploded. "That's what he told everyone, but do you know the name of Neon's doctor? No you don't, because he didn't exist. Neon was a liar. A pathological liar. And I'll tell you something else. I don't think there's a brother. I think it was all in Neon's mind. I never saw any brother and, Mae, I was a hell of a lot closer to Neon then you were!"

"Stop braggin'," said Mae, "it's unbecomin'."

Connery ignored her. "Tell me, Villon, have you any proof these orgies took place?"

"None."

"Have you any proof Neon wasn't killed in Griffith Park?"

"None."

"Have you anything but a suspicion as to who might have killed Neon?"

"Stop right there, Connery."

Mallory relaxed. He had feared Villon was painting himself into a corner. Connery was being astonishingly fearless in challenging Herb Villon. Mallory didn't like the way the conversation was going until now. Hazel was back scribbling in the notebook. Villon was taking control again.

Villon said calmly, "My suspicions have a lovely way of coming home to roost. All my suspicions concerning Neon's murderer are concrete. They're adding up. His murderer is going to slip up the way all murderers slip up sooner or later. Some murderers loosen their tie and unbutton their shirt collar when things are getting a little hot for them."

Connery slammed a fist on the table. "Are you accusing me of murdering Neon?"

Villon said with a smile, "You're the best candidate I've got."

"You've got nothing on me. You can't prove anything. You're just a big bag of wind. I've had enough of your crap!" He pushed his chair back and Superman caught it. Connery rudely shoved Superman aside and began pushing his way backstage.

Mae said to Villon, "I think you've got his dander up. Say, Agnes, did he always have such a short fuse?"

Unruffled, having just lit another cigarette, Agnes said, "It's Hallowe'en. These parties always have him on edge. Anything can happen and it usually does. It's a little early but I can assure you, some faces are going to be slapped and scratched, a few

168

brawls will break out, there'll be screaming hysterics and possibly the arrival of a squad car or two. And on top of that, Herb more or less tells him he thinks he murdered Neon."

"Now just a minute," said Mae, as Superman, apparently bored with it all, wandered off. "Herb did not say Milton murdered Neon."

"He might just as well have." She looked at Villon, who was wondering whether to eat his sandwich or shoot it. "There wasn't much subtlety emanating from our detective's mouth." Villon chuckled. "He was doing the job he came here to do. He came here to shake Milton up, and, Mr. Villon, you certainly shook him up."

"Weren't you a little shook up too, Agnes?" asked Mae.

"Why should I be?"

"You work for Connery."

"I helped with the party tonight."

"Agnes, I think you been helpin' with a lot of other things. Now don't interrupt me. For a long time I been wonderin' how you support yourself. How come you never put the touch on me?" She wished Beverly would stop looking at Jim Mallory as though he might be dessert. And she was positive Seymour Steel Cheeks was flirting with someone at the bar, but she couldn't tell who.

"I have private means."

"Ain't you lucky. Well, Herb, what happens next?"

Before Villon could answer, Simon LeGrand came hurrying to the table, the snakes in his wig flopping about comically. He knelt at Herb's side and said, "There's been a murder. In the garden. I've got a guard on the door so no one can go out there."

"Well, I'm goin' out there," said Mae, "I want to see for myself. Don't try to stop me, Herb." Villon signaled to Mallory to join him and Mae. Villon said to the others, "Stay here." Hazel Dickson was having none of it. She hurried to join the exodus to the garden.

Milton Connery had hired about half a dozen private guards to police the party and keep order. He did it every Hallowe'en and every New Year's Eve as a means of seeing that the parties stayed on the right side of the law. Tonight the six guards wore costumes and melted into the crowd. The one guarding the door to the garden was dressed as Charlie Chaplin. He looked absolutely ludicrous. He knew who Villon and Mallory were because Simon LeGrand had told him they were on the premises. Mae chucked the guard under the chin as she sauntered into the garden and asked, "How's Paulette?" Actress Paulette Goddard was Chaplin's paramour of the moment and possibly his wife.

Villon and Mallory knelt on either side of Billie Doux. They turned her on her back. Villon said, "Same modus operandi as the others. The jugular and the knife to the heart. Hazel, find a phone and call the precinct. Get the coronor and some backup."

Simon LeGrand said nervously, "I better find Milton and tell him. He's not going to like this."

"Wait a minute, not so fast. Do you know her?" asked Villon.

"You sure it's a woman?" asked Mallory.

"It's a woman," Mae said quietly. "She was a nice young woman. Her name's Billie Doux." Hazel made a mental note of the name as she went in search of a phone. "She was the production secretary on my pitcher. She told me she was comin' dressed as me and I begged her not to. I don't know why, but I had a feelin' somethin' bad was goin' to happen tonight."

Simon LeGrand said, "Please, Mr. Villon. I've got to tell Milton." Villon waved him away. Simon hurried off muttering a variety of unpleasant epithets under his breath.

Mallory said to Villon, "Herb, he could still be inside. He could be in there stalking his next victim."

"He's got a lot to choose from tonight. His head must be swimming."

"Damn it! Beverly!" Mae exploded. "She's in there unprotected!"

Villon barred her way. "Take it easy, Mae, not so fast. She's got Timony and Steel Cheeks in there with her. The killer won't try anything in that crowd. He killed Billie because she was dumb enough to come out here alone for a smoke."

Mae said indignantly, "She ignored my warnin'."

"Maybe she didn't hear it. Possibly she was already out here when you were giving your little speech."

"Yeah, you're probably right." She stared at the corpse. "Lookin' at Billie, it's beginnin' to really hit home. It's gettin' to me. So this is what it looks like. The punctured neck. The bleeding wound in the heart. This is how the others looked when they were found. God damn it, why is this guy after me?"

A bartender directed Hazel to a telephone. As she went looking for it, she tripped and started to fall. Two strong arms caught her and kept her from hitting the floor. Hazel said gratefully to her rescuer, "Thank you, Superman," and continued on her way in search of the telephone.

Villon was speaking to the Charlie Chaplin guard. "How many of you are working this madhouse?"

"There's six of us."

"Can you round them up?"

"I can try."

"Go get them. Jim, take the door while my friend here rounds up his buddies."

Jim took his position in the doorway while Mae continued to fret about Beverly. "I should have made her stay in the East. This bookin' was a big mistake. I'll strangle Jim Timony for gettin' it for her. If she gets herself murdered, I'll never forgive myself."

"Mae," said Villon, "you're forgetting you have bodyguards at your table with your sister."

Mae slapped a hip and stamped a foot. "I must be losin' my marbles. Well, thanks for remindin' me. That's a relief. Well, while we're waitin', why don't we look for some clues? What's that cigarette doin' next to the body?"

Villon picked it up. "Probably Billie's. It has lipstick on it."

"In this place and this party you call that a clue? You see anybody tonight who *ain't* wearin' lipstick?" She sauntered about, hands on hip, muttering about Villon's naïveté. "What about footprints?"

Villon mimiced her badly. "In this place at this party?"

"Okay, so what about the ring? Maybe he dropped the ring."

Villon was kneeling and examining the hem of Billie's costume. "He didn't drop it. He wiped the blood off here."

Mae said, "How uncouth, wipin' blood off a ring with your victim's hem. Y'know, I wore this thing in *Belle of the Nineties*. Billie got it out of wardrobe. Oh, hell, wait till Desdemona and Goneril find out she's been murdered. The girls were very fond of each other."

Mallory was blocking the doorway to Robinson Crusoe and Friday. Crusoe remonstrated, "We were told to ask for Detective Villon."

Herb said, "You two of the guards?"

"That's us. How can we help?"

"Round up all the Mae West impersonators. Tell your buddies to do the same."

"Our guys aren't easy to find. Nate, the one doing Charlie Chaplin, he found us at the bar. I haven't seen any of the other three for the past hour."

"Well, keep looking for them." He jerked a thumb in Billie's direction. "Her killer might still be here, and he's just nuts enough to try and kill again. Take the impersonators backstage and keep them there. I've got backup on its way and they'll take over when they get here. Get moving." Crusoe and Friday hurried out, not too eager to plunge into the mass of inhumanity packing the nightclub.

Agnes Darwin was standing, staring down at Milton Connery seated behind the desk, when Simon LeGrand hurried in without knocking, an infraction Connery found intolerable, but tonight Simon didn't give a damn. There was a stiff in the garden. Word of her murder would soon spread like syphilis, and Simon wasn't looking forward to the possibility of mass hysteria. "Milton! Milton!" he shouted.

Agnes said much too calmly, "You're making enough noise to wake the dead."

Simon was fighting a rising hysteria. "But there's been a murder in the garden and—"

Agnes waved him quiet. "I know. I overheard you telling Villon. I came to tell Milton. Milton wouldn't listen." She pointed at Connery. Simon came closer.

"Oh, oh, oh," said Simon, "Oh, oh, oh."

"Well," said Agnes, "I suppose oh, oh, oh is better then screaming."

There was a puncture mark above the jugular vein. He had also been stabbed in the heart. But what neither one of them would ever forget was the look of sheer terror on his face.

"But—but—but—" sputtered Simon, "he's not an impersonator. Why kill Milton?"

"Oh, Simon," Agnes said as she took him by the arm and led the way out of the office in search of Villon and Mallory, "there are loads of reasons to kill Milton. I could name quite a few myself. And don't look at me like that, I'm a witch, not a vampire. I don't own any fangs, I find them most unbecoming. Let's go to the garden and tell Mr. Villon he's hit the jackpot tonight. Not one murder but two murders. Simon, do you suppose he'll think that's just dandy?"

SIXTEEN

AGNES WAS IN MIND OF THE ancient Greek custom of killing the messenger who brought bad news. The look on Villon's face almost convinced her she and Simon were doomed.

Mae, hands on hips, a look of exasperation on her face, said wryly, "Ain't we lucky. A double header." She shook her head and clucked her tongue. "You gotta hand it to this killer. He sure treads where angels fear. Herb, are your feet frozen to the cement? Ain't you goin' to pay Connery a visit?"

"What's the rush? He's not going anywhere. Jim, you go have a look. Here comes Charlie Chaplin, he can go back on the door." Hazel Dickson was behind Charlie Chaplin.

Hazel told Villon, "They're on their way. Where's Mallory going in such a rush?"

"Hazel," said Villon, "this is your lucky night. I assume you phoned the news of Billie Doux's murder to the *Times.*"

"Have you ever known me to miss a golden opportunity?" she rasped.

"No, sweetheart, and another golden opportunity awaits." He told her of Connery's murder. Hazel yelped and disappeared in the direction of the telephone.

"Herb." Mae's voice was subdued. She looked troubled. "Herb, I think the killer was standing right by our table when

174

you were baitin' Connery. The guy in the Superman costume wearin' that cockamamie mask with the red spangles. He was eavesdroppin' on us. I could feel his eyes on me. He just stood there, the brazen bastard. I saw him leave us just after Connery made his big exit. Don't you get it? He followed Connery and killed him. You as much as told everyone Connery killed Neon, and Superman is Neon's brother. He's got to be!'' She was all worked up, excited, her adrenaline bubbling. "Simon! Go get Selma Hamilton Burr. He's my black bodyguard. Tell him to scour this place and find a guy in a Superman costume.''

Villon rasped, "Get going, Simon.''

Simon got going while thinking, *Connery is dead*. Who takes over the club? Who'll handle tonight's receipts? Who are his associates? Agnes would know. He'd have to talk to Agnes. Maybe strike a deal with her. With Connery out of the way, he didn't have to give an honest count on the night's take. And what a take! The biggest since he came to work at the club. He saw Selma. He was on the dance floor with Goneril and Desdemona. The three were doing a cakewalk, egged on by a circle of rowdy patrons. Simon pushed his way onto the dance floor. He shouted to Selma that Mae had a chore for him to do. Mae's name was magic. Selma left the dance floor with Simon, saying "If Superman's still here, I'll find him.''

Simon saw Robinson Crusoe and Friday shepherding several angry Mae Wests backstage. Jason the bartender caught Simon's eye and pointed to the entrance. Several plainclothesmen were entering with the coroner. Simon intercepted them and led them to the garden where Villon exhaled a sigh of relief. Hazel Dickson stopped at Mae's table to tell Timony and Beverly of Connery's murder.

Beverly gasped. "What happens to my opening tomorrow night?'' She beseeched Timony. "Who takes over for Connery?''

"Your guess is as good as mine,'' said Timony. "Maybe Simon LeGrand knows.'' He instructed Dudley Van Helsing and Salvatore Puccini to keep a sharp watch on Beverly and wondered where Seymour Steel Cheeks had disappeared to.

175

In the garden, the coroner was kneeling and examining the body. Villon assigned some of his men to help Selma search for a man in a Superman disguise. As Hazel rejoined them, Villon ordered her and Mae back to the table.

"What's there to do at the table? Knowin' Beverly the way I know her, if she's heard Connery's croaked—"

"She's heard it from me," interjected Hazel.

"There you go. Everything's hit the fan. Bev is probably frettin' about maybe not openin' tomorrow night."

"She is," said Hazel.

Mae said to Hazel, "It's nice to know you sometimes come in handy." She said to Villon, "And if there's no openin', I couldn't be happier. I'm shippin' Beverly back East."

The coroner got to his feet. "Nothing more I can do here."

"Yes, there is. There's another stiff in an office backstage. It's Milton Connery, who runs this joint."

"Ah!" said the coroner, feigning bliss, "two for the price of one. I had no idea vampires enjoyed working overtime."

"Come on, Mallory's with the stiff."

"Murder makes strange bedfellows," muttered the coroner as he tailed Villon out of the garden.

Agnes Darwin had stood to one side with her arms folded wondering what was in store for her with Connery dead. It was as though Mae were reading her mind. "Well, Agnes, get out your crystal ball and see what the future holds now that your benefactor's gone to his very just reward."

"Milton was not my benefactor." The ice in her voice was unmistakable.

"Okay, you go to your church and I'll go to mine. So who takes over the operation here? Simon LeGrand? He seems competent enough. Who's behind the operation?"

"As far as I know, it was all Milton's."

"Oh, yeah? No silent partners? The way the mob's been musclin' into this town the past couple of years, I'm sure they didn't ignore Milton." She snapped her fingers. "I'll bet I can find it in his office." She hip-rolled her way in the direction of Connery's office. She saw three of her facsimiles being herded toward the backstage by two men dressed as Peter Pan and Little Lord Fauntleroy. Lord Fauntleroy was bow-legged and waddled. So much for private guards, thought Mae. Agnes was following her saying Mae had no right to go through Connery's private papers. Connery had a lawyer who had Connery's power of attorney, should anything happen to him. Mae let Agnes prattle on, the words falling on almost deaf ears.

Backstage was a cornucopia of Mae West imitators in various stages of rage, outrage, and high spirits. They were mostly men of various ages in drag. There were a few women, and they looked dispirited. Charlie Chaplin was convincing them that they'd been herded together for their own safety. After he told them Billie Doux had been found murdered in the garden, one Mae Westian drawl boldly inquired, "Didn't she have the brains to stay out of the bushes?"

Mae entered and said to Agnes, "Pernt me to Connery's office and don't horse around." Agnes indicated a door on Mae's left. It was open and Mae saw Villon, Mallory, and the coroner. She entered the office and was taken completely by surprise by seeing Father Riggs standing near a steel filing cabinet.

"Why, Father Wally, what are you doing here?" He looked like a fish out of water, which he certainly was.

"Mae, how good to see you. I had a phone call asking me to come here to give last rites. I haven't a clue as to whether this gentleman"—indicating Connery—"was a Catholic."

"Agnes?" Mae thought Agnes looked as though she could use a blood transfusion. "What was Connery besides a bum and a killer?"

"He wasn't a religious man," said Agnes, wondering how long it would take for the torch she carried for Connery to extinguish itself.

Mae looked exasperated. "I knew it was gonna be one of those nights. Well, Father—"

Father Riggs interrupted. "Perhaps the person in the garden . . ."

Mae took a beat before responding. "Billie Doux? I can't say if she was Catholic or not. Maybe my girls know. They were very friendly with her." Simon was standing in the doorway, anxious for some words with Agnes. "Simon! Did you phone Father Riggs here to come do his last rites routine?"

"I don't know Father Riggs. I've never met him before."

"Would you know if Connery was a Catholic?"

"We never discussed religion."

"This person who phoned you, Father, was it a man or a woman?"

"Well, frankly, Mae, I couldn't really tell. I tend to think it might have been a masculine voice although it was a bit high pitched."

"There's a lotta verses around here that are a bit high pitched. Say, Simon, find my girls and see if they know if Billie Doux was Catholic."

Simon said anxiously, "I have to talk to Agnes."

"Agnes ain't goin' anywhere, are you, Agnes?"

"I'll be here," said Agnes.

"Y'see, Simon, Agnes will be here. I mean, as long as we've got a priest on the premises, we might as well make some use of him." Simon departed and Mae smiled at Father Riggs. "Well, Father, how's business?"

Villon was also surprised to see Father Riggs, having been too preoccupied with the coroner to notice the priest's arrival. "Why, Father Riggs, how nice to see you again, although not under very pleasant circumstances. I thought you were one of the club patrons in costume for the party. Though dressing as a priest at a Halloween ball I should think would be in very bad taste."

"Oh, I don't think so. I noticed a few nuns out there and if I'm not mistaken, there's a rather large woman dressed as the pope. I also saw a witch doctor."

"Witch doctors don't count," said Mae. "From what I've been told they ain't got no acceptable denomination. Would you excuse me a moment, Father, I'd like a few cherce words with my friend Herb here. Let me lead you outside, Herb." She rolled her eyes and said through a sly smile, "Or would you rather I led you astray? Either way it's a short trip."

Father Riggs said to Agnes, who was looking nervous as she applied a cigarette lighter to her cigarette, "My dear Miss Darwin, forgive my saying so, you look as though you could use some words of comfort."

"I could use some words," she said after exhaling, "but comfort isn't one of them."

He shifted gears. "Isn't Mae West an amazing woman?"

"Yes she is," said Agnes, looking and sounding grim.

"She doesn't seem in the least bit fazed by these vampire murders. But why would the killer slay Mr. Connery in the same way he killed the impersonators?"

"Maybe because the implements were convenient. I doubt if there was more than half an hour between Billie's death and Milton's."

It was Mallory's turn to acknowledge the priest's surprising presence. Father Riggs again explained what he was doing here and Mallory said, "Now that's a bit queer."

"The right expression for tonight's festivities," said Agnes.

Mallory ignored her. "I hope someone hasn't played a cruel joke."

Father Riggs was perplexed. "But why call me? True, my church is nearby and convenient but . . . oh, well, no harm done. I don't get much excitement in my life, and this is quite fascinating. It's like being a part of the morning headlines."

The coroner said to Mallory, "I'll have the meat wagon brought around the back. I don't think it's a good idea to transport the bodies through the club."

Mae overheard him as she returned with Villon. "It wouldn't matter. That gang out there would think it was part of the show." She asked Villon, "What are you gonna do with all my impersonators huddled out there? I can hear them growin' impatient. Why don't you let them go back and enjoy themselves? I don't think this here vampire would be dumb enough to strike again tonight."

Villon reminded her, "You yourself said catastrophes usually come in threes."

"Well, I ain't always right," Mae said grandly. "Anyway, we don't have to be afraid of no vampire with a priest here. That crucifix around his neck will scare him off, right, Father?"

"It usually does in the movies," he replied through a laugh, "but as I told you the other day, I don't believe in the existence of vampires."

Simon LeGrand returned, out of breath. "You're in luck, Father, Billie Doux was a Catholic."

Mae said, "How nice. So the evenin' wasn't a total waste at all."

"I'll attend to her now, while there's time."

Villon said, "Simon, would you—" He watched Father Riggs leaving the office, heading for the garden. Simon was waiting for Villon to finish the sentence.

Simon asked, "Would I what?"

Villon said, "What?"

Simon said, "You said, 'Simon, would you . . .' and I'm waiting for the rest of it."

Mae said swiftly, "Would you open these files, or aren't they locked?"

"If they are, the keys are in the top drawer. He keeps everything in the top drawer."

"I'll bet I know what he keeps in them files."

Agnes spoke up. "Mae, let me give you some advice. Opening those files is like opening Pandora's box."

"I never met any Pandora and if I did, I don't remember openin' her box."

Agnes explained the Pandora legend to her. Mae exclaimed, "So that's the broad who started all the troubles in this world. Well, my mother taught Beverly and me not to stick our two cents where it's not wanted. But what's this got to do with openin' them files?"

Agnes turned to Villon. "Herb, you can guess what those files contain."

"So can I," said Mae, "and as a tax-payin' citizen I got a right to know what's in them files."

It was Villon's turn to put his hands on his hips. "Mae, I don't get the connection. What's paying your taxes got to do with your poking around in the files?"

"Mmmmmm, I'd like to have a look at some of them pitchers. I'm sure they're very interestin', and I'm always interested in anything interestin'."

Agnes said to Mae, "Connery's dead. Let what's in those files die with him." She said to Villon, "Herb, I know what's there and what's there could destroy a lot of people if it falls into the wrong hands. There's a large barbecue in the garden. Have someone light it and burn everything in those files."

"Now wait a minute." Mae looked suspicious. "Why do I think you're lookin' to see stuff go up in smoke that has something to do with you?"

"I've got nothing to be afraid of. I never participated in the orgies. I admit helping to set them up, arranging for the participants. Yes, Neon was a part of them. Connery paid me handsome fees for my help and I don't mind telling you"—her voice began to choke—"I'll miss those fees."

Mae said softly and sympathetically, "Agnes, you could get a tan from that torch you're carryin'." She crossed to Agnes and put an arm around the troubled woman's shoulder. "Boy, you're one hell of a witch. You haven't got the brains to cast a spell over yourself and give yourself some peace and quiet like I get when I'm soakin' in my Olympic-size bathtub, which I wish I was doin' right now." She diverted her attention to Villon. "Whaddya say, Herb? You gonna burn the stuff?"

Villon said to Agnes, "Agnes, Jim Mallory and I will go through the file drawers. We have to. We can't destroy somebody else's property without first seeing what is there. There might be something important that you don't know about."

Agnes said, "What about Hazel Dickson?"

Villon said, "What about her?"

Agnes said, "You won't tell her about what you'll find in that cabinet?"

"Positively not," said Villon. "She's done well enough for herself tonight. I wouldn't want to spoil her. Come on in, boys." Two morgue attendants entered with a stretcher.

Mae headed for the door. "I'm goin' back to the table. You comin', Agnes?"

"I'd like to. I don't want to be alone." Agnes waited.

Mae turned and looked at her. "Well, come on, for cryin' out loud, or do you expect an engraved invitation?"

Beverly West was boiling mad when Mae and Agnes returned. "Where have you been, Mae? Leaving me alone all this time."

"Ain't my bodyguards been entertainin' you?" Selma Hamilton Burr was back sitting with Salvatore Puccini and Dudley Van Helsing. "What's the matter with you lunkheads? Don't any of you know any dirty jokes? Wait a minute. There's somebody I want you to meet, Beverly." She called out, hoping she could be heard above the clamor. "Father Wally! Over here!" He saw Mae and joined the table.

"My, isn't it a bit wild in here?" Mae indicated he sit next to her.

"You mean that striptease artist on the bar?" She asked her bodyguards, "Why is it the worst physiques like to bare them in public? Oh, Beverly, forgive me, you haven't been introduced to Father Riggs. Beverly, this is Father Riggs. Father, this is my sister Beverly."

"The resemblance is remarkable," commented the priest.

"Tell me, Father, have you ever been in this den of iniquity before?" asked Mae sweetly.

"Oh, my, no. This is quite a new experience for me."

"You could use it as the text of next Sunday's sermon."

"I see no reason to. It's just a party. Everyone seems to be enjoying themselves."

"You know what they say in the public library, Father. Don't judge a book by its covers. There's a lot of hidden heartbreak here tonight. A lot of these guys in drag were very close to the murder victims. Those brave kids dressed up like me know they're takin' their own lives in their hands. This vampire nut struck twice tonight. About Connery I got no regrets. He was a rotten skunk. And a skunk is just a rat wearin' a fur coat. Billie Doux was something else. She was a sweet lady hopin' and waitin' for someone to love her. Why she thought she'd find him in this jernt tonight, I'll never know. All she found was Superman, much, I'm sure, to her regret.''

"Superman? What Superman?" Beverly had her compact open and was repairing her face, a face that some brave soul would one day tell her was beyond repair.

"You been so busy tryin' to make time with Jim Mallory, you didn't notice. Talk about Jim, where's Timony? And where's my Indian?"

Beverly said with a girlish squeal, "Oh, I sure do like your Indian!"

"Oh, yeah? Well, don't get your hopes up too high. I ain't no Indian giver." She spotted Timony at the bar with Desdemona and Goneril. "There's Timony, with my girls. Ah, the poor things. Just look at them. All broken up over Billie's murder. I hope they didn't see the morgue boys removin' the cold cuts.''

"Would it help if I gave them some words of consolation?" asked Father Riggs.

"A couple of brandy Alexanders would work better. Timony's handling them. He's been like a father to them. They'll miss him when he goes back East."

"He's leaving?" asked Father Riggs.

"Yeah, Father. When you gotta go, you gotta go. There's Seymour at the bar with Hazel Dickson. He's talkin' and she's scribblin'. I hope he ain't revealin' any of my state secrets. If he is, I'll put him in a state and I don't mean Oregon. Now, as we were sayin', Father, don't judge a book by its covers."

"You were saying that," he corrected.

Mae smiled. "Thank you, Father, for not takin' the words out of my mouth."

Beverly snapped the compact shut and popped it into her purse. "You were sayin' somethin' about Superman, Mae. What Superman?"

"Why, the one Villon and me think is the murderer.''

"Oh, come off it! You said the murderer dresses like a vampire."

"Well, he didn't tonight and very smart of him. Very smart man, this murderer, Father, very smart man. If I was wearin' a hat tonight, I'd tip it to him."

"I'm all at sea," said Father Riggs. "You're going much too fast for me."

"That's what a lot of other guys have said to me from time to time. Fortunately, a lot of them caught up." She smiled. "I'll take it slower. Before Connery was killed, he was sittin' right where you are, Father, and Herb Villon was givin' him a hard time. This here guy in a wild Superman disguise with a weird mask to cover his face stood right next to the table makin' like he was watching the goings-on on the dance floor, but what he was really doin' was listenin' to the talk between Villon and Connery. Villon just about laid it out for Connery that Villon knew he murdered Neon Light but didn't have the proof with which to run him in. Connery got mad and got up, throwin' his chair back. This here Superman caught it, by the way, which was very nice of him. Everythin' else ain't. Connery went back to his office and I saw Superman also head in that direction. Billie Doux already was dead. When Herb examined her body, which Simon LeGrand found, there were bloodstains on the hem of her gown. Superman must have wiped one of his weapons clean."

"Why would Billie's killer be Superman?"

"Connery was killed the same way the other five were killed: puncture marks above the jugular and a knife to the heart."

Beverly said nervously, "Must you be so graphic, Sis?"

"Come off it. We seen worse when Pop was gettin' beat up in the ring." She returned to the priest. "Superman's our best bet as the killer. For another thing, he beat a hasty retreat out of here. There are private guards on duty tonight and Villon set them out to look for Superman. Not a sign of him. If he was just another party guest, why go home so early? The evenin's still young. It's not yet midnight." She said in an aside to Agnes, "Your favorite hour." Agnes had signaled a waiter and requested a fresh bottle of champagne. "Go easy on the bubbly, Agnes," cautioned Mae, but warmly. "It could make you dizzy and you might fall off your broomstick and hurt yourself." She patted the priest's hand. "Am I makin' sense to you, Father?"

"It all seems quite logical if it's so. I still don't see why he would want to kill Mr. Connery."

"He killed Mr. Connery because he believed Herb Villon's suspicion that Connery murdered Neon Light. And we think the killer in the Superman costume is Neon Light's brother."

"How extraordinary!" The priest accepted a glass of champagne. "Can you prove this?"

Mae didn't answer him. Herb Villon and Jim Mallory were returning to the table. She leaned back in her chair and asked, "I suppose I missed somethin' real good."

"Mae," said Villon, "I think what we had destroyed would have brought a blush even to your cheeks."

"Oh, I don't know about that. I think the last time I blushed was when I was propositioned by Jimmy Walker when he was mayor of New York. At the time he made me blush, he was sittin' in Helen Morgan's nightclub with his wife and his mistress. Now that really took *chutzpah*."

"And what is *chutzpah*?" asked Father Riggs.

"Nerve, Father, just plain nerve, sometimes of a very outrageous nature. Like Superman tonight. Two killin's in a row within a half hour of each other. Now if that ain't a perfect example of *chutzpah*, I'd like to know what is?"

Simon LeGrand joined them and said to Agnes, "I still need to talk to you, Agnes."

"About what? Milton's dead." Her voice rose. "What's there to talk about? His funeral. It'll be a small affair, I can assure you. There aren't that many around who'll mourn Milton Connery. I'll arrange the mortuary. There's one on Fairfax across the street from the Witches' Brew. It's nondenominational. As for his personal effects, whether he left a will, I'll phone his lawyer in the morning. He'll take care of everything.

As for the Tailspin, I suppose there's enough cash on hand to go on with Beverly's opening tomorrow night."

Beverly spoke and surprised Mae, who was glad to hear the words. "I think it would be sacrilegious to open tomorrow night what with Mr. Connery's murder and all. No, I won't open. Cancel it. Don't you agree, Sis?"

Mae leaned back with a lovely smile. "Beverly, I couldn't agree more. Well, Herb Villon, we've got a lot to talk about tomorrow, don't we?"

"We sure do, Mae, we sure do."

SEVENTEEN

FOR A LOT OF PEOPLE, THE next day was a truly black Friday.
Goldie Rothfeld sat at the kitchen table sipping hot black coffee and staring at a slice of her own coffee cake. The rabbi had
come in very late the previous night. He'd been coming in late
rather often these past two months. Was there another woman?
Would Morris cheat on her? She considered awakening him
and asking him and just as quickly decided not to. If there's
another woman, let it run its course. The phone bell nagged and
she crossed to the wall.

"Hello?"

"Could I speak to the rabbi, please?" It was a woman.

"He's asleep. On Friday the rabbi sleeps late. If you give me
your number I'll have him phone you."

"Am I speaking to his wife?"

"Yes. And who am I speaking to?"

"I'm Madame Kvitcherdicker, his vocal coach."

Goldie's heart skipped a beat. "Vocal coach? Since when?"

"Hasn't he told you? Oh, I could bite my tongue. He probably wanted to surprise you. He said you wanted him to resume
his singing career. And my dear Mrs. Rothfeld, how right you
are. He has a glorious instrument. He must share it with the
world. It certainly won't interfere with his rabbinical duties.

There are many other rabbis who play professional dates. You've heard of Yosele Rosenblatt?"

"Of course. He's the best."

"Your husband's better, take my word for it." Goldie was on cloud nine. "We worked into the wee hours last night until I got a death threat from a neighbor. Now, Mrs. Rabbi . . ."

"It's Goldie. Call me Goldie." Her voice dripped with joy.

"Oh, Goldie, we must meet soon. But don't give it away that you know he's studying with me. We were planning on working again Sunday night but I can't make it. We'll have to set another date." She paused. "Oh, dear. If you tell him I called, then he'll know that you know and there won't be any surprise. Do you love surprises? I loathe them. Anyway, why don't I call back later? Will an hour be too soon?"

"That should be just right. You really think he's good?"

"Goldie, you are appropriately named, because you are married to a potential gold mine. Soon I'll be arranging auditions for him, and you mark my words with a red pencil, that rich Jewish Hollywood crowd will be falling all over themselves to book him. And those gorgeous looks of his don't hurt any either. My dear, if I was twenty years younger, would I be giving you a hard time!" Her voice cascaded into a waterfall of laughter, and from the sound of her, Goldie envisioned a woman of extraordinary weight.

Half an hour later, wearing his familiar tattered bathrobe and his worn bedroom slippers, Morris Rothfeld shuffled into the kitchen, yawning and scratching his head. Goldie threw her arms around him and gave him a sloppy kiss.

"Please, Goldie, not on an empty stomach."

"I love you, Morris Rothfeld, I love you love you love you."

His eyes widened with amazement. "How come? You heard I inherited money?"

Enrobed in a harlequin peignoir, Mae West opened the door to admit Herb Villon and Jim Mallory. Villon asked, "The great lady answering the door herself?"

She wiggled her way to the sideboard. "The great lady had no cherce. I think Desdemona and Goneril died in their sleep. Or else they're in a coma what with all the drinkin' they did at the club and all the wailin' for Billie when we got home."

"I suppose Beverly is still in the arms of Morpheus?" asked Villon.

"No, handsome, she slept alone last night." She indicated the coffee and rolls on the sideboard. "Help yourselves. It's a little sparse but it's the best I could do." She swayed to the throne chair where a cup of black coffee awaited her attention on an end table. "I ain't seen the papers yet. Did last night make headlines? I didn't notice no reporters or photographers."

"Hazel was a one-woman army. She scooped everybody in town." He poured coffee for himself and Mallory.

"Nice lady, Hazel, if a little ditsy. You plannin' on marryin' her, Herb?"

"What for?"

"Ain't you in love with her?"

"Do I have to be?"

"You don't have to be anything. I've got a woman's unnatural curiosity. If there's no payoff in the cards for her, why's she stickin' around?"

"Because if I must say so myself," said Villon, "I'm about the best she'll ever get in this town."

Mae tsk'ed and said, "And they say I'm an egomaniac. Compared to you, Herb Villon, I'm Snow White minus the dwarfs. I hear activity in the kitchen. The ladies are alive."

Desdemona appeared. "Miss Mae, there's no Bromo Seltzer. If we don't have some soon, we will die."

"Serves you right, the way the two of you drank and carried on last night. Phone the drugstore, they'll send it up. And while you're at it, tell them to send up some smellin' salts."

"You feelin' faint?" asked Desdemona in a monotone.

"No, I ain't feelin' faint, but there could be an emergency later."

"Why?"

"I'll send you a letter by special delivery! Now beat it!" Mae smiled at the detectives as Desdemona picked her way slowly and delicately back to the kitchen. "It's goin' to be a real rough day around here." She looked at her diamond-encrusted wrist-watch. "I got a date to go to church." They waited for her to continue. "I phoned Father Riggs to tell him I'm comin' in for confession. He dropped the phone. When he picked it up, I gave him a song and dance about bein' depressed by all these killin's and needin' some comfortin'. He offered to come here but I said no, today I'd like to do it accordin' to the rules. No special privileges. I told him Seymour would pilot me there in the Rolls, otherwise I'd be alone. Well, whaddya think, Herb? Do you think he knows we know?"

"I think he's tired of the game. Also, he's a man of the cloth."

"Seems to me that slipped his mind a long time ago. Poor son of a bitch. With those looks he could have been a movie star. If he hadn't have come back to the club last night, he'd still be on the loose. Do you think he wanted to be caught?"

"You've heard that old one about the murderer always re-turning to the scene of the crime? Well, in this case, I think he realized killing Milton Connery in the club was a mistake. Killing anyone in the club was a mistake. What's wrong, Mae?"

She suppressed a shudder. "He had me right there. He was standin' over me. He could have settled it once and for all. You really believe he wants to kill me because I convinced Neon to go on with his career?"

"Absolutely. The man's a lunatic."

Mae's hands were upturned, showing her palms. She was incredulous. "I ain't known any priests before who were luna-tics! How will he face his maker after all he's done?" She thought and then answered her question herself. "He'll proba-bly throw himself on the mercy of the court as an orphan." She asked Mallory to get her some fresh coffee from the sideboard. "And killin' them facsimiles of me, not because they needed to die but because he wanted to frighten the hell out of me." Her eyes met Villon's. "And the Williamsons? That was him too?"

"At first my money was on Connery. Dvorack must have told him they were planning to hire a private dick to continue the investigation. But then I thought of Riggs's hatred of them too because they encouraged Neon. Anyway, Connery's dead and out of it. As for Father Riggs, it's Judgment Day."

"I'll wear somethin' subdued in keepin' with the occasion. You know, I'm always sayin' to my friends, 'See you in church'. Well now I'm goin' and it ain't even Sunday. Come on in, James." Timony nodded to the detectives. "You still plannin' to take off tomorrow mornin'?"

"I said I'd leave when the murderer is caught and you're out of danger."

"He ain't caught yet. There's many a slip twixt the cup and the lip. And here's slipping beauty."

Beverly entered briskly. "Hello everybody, what a glorious morning!"

"The girls in the kitchen don't think so," said Mae. "There's coffee and rolls on the sideboard. It's all I could scrape up. Unless Goneril's got some stuff hidden away in case of a famine."

Beverly said to Villon, "Will I be in danger if I borrow a bodyguard and go shopping at Bullock's?"

Villon said, "Give it a couple of hours."

"Oh, heavens, it'll take me longer then that to get ready! These rolls look stale."

Mae was on her way to her boudoir. "There are a lot of things around here that look stale." She said to Villon and Mallory, "I'll be ready in a jiffy."

The circles under Father Riggs's eyes were deep and dark. It had been a sleepless night. A night of constant prayer and pleading to the Almighty for forgiveness. He found a picture of his baby brother Mickey at the bottom of his desk drawer and placed it on the mantel of the fireplace in his living room. He lit a votive candle and set it against the photo of his brother. He wept bitterly. Then the phone call from Mae West. Mae West. MAE WEST. Yes, Mae, confess. Confess your multitude of sins. Confess, Mae. You're as responsible for these killings as I am. If you hadn't interfered, if you hadn't led Mickey astray, he'd be alive today. Those infernal impersonators wouldn't have had to die. The Williamsons wouldn't be dead. He was at the desk staring into the open top drawer. Staring at the knife reposing on a velvet cloth. Staring at the bat's head ring with its deadly fangs. MAE WEST.

The buzzer told him someone was waiting for him in the confessional. It couldn't be her. It was too early. He dried his eyes. Slowly he left the apartment and entered his side of the confessional.

"You there, Father?" It was him again. The nut case. Brothers under the skin.

"Yes, my son."

"Forgive me, Father, for I have sinned. But you know that already if you read this morning's papers. I sure gave that party last night some extra added attractions. You know, sometimes I confuse myself. I don't know why I killed that man Canary."

"Connery."

"Yeah, right, Connery. Doesn't seem to me as he had any connection to Mae West. But, oh well, in for a penny, in for a pound. You know, Father, I keep wondering, ain't you itching to expose me to the cops?"

"Not at all," he said softly. "Perhaps you don't realize you've been doing a service to mankind."

"Yeah? You mean like I'm a scientist, something like that?"

"Milton Connery was a terrible man."

"You knew him?" He was startled.

"I knew of him." His head was throbbing. He felt in his pocket. The ring and the knife were there. Perhaps he should murder this fool. Put him out of his misery. On the other hand, he might be enjoying himself. Domiciled in his fool's paradise. Oh, why doesn't he go away?

"Father? Why are you so quiet? Am I boring you?"

He wanted to scream, Yes, yes, yes, you all bore me, is this what lies in store for me for the rest of my life? Listening to the confessions of blithering idiots like you, listening to old ladies chatter away not because they feel the need to confess anything but because they're lonely and want somebody to talk to, listening to religious fanatics who drone on and on about how they don't think they're giving the best of themselves to Jesus. And Jesus. What of Him? I have betrayed Him, as I have betrayed myself. He heard himself say, "Fifty Hail Marys!"

"You crazy? I mean, forgive me, Father, but—"

"Fifty Hail Marys! Now go on, get the hell out of here!"

Father Wally went back to his apartment. He leaned against the door gasping for breath. MAE WEST. He had to make ready. This was it. The moment he had been waiting for. He removed the knife and ring from the pocket and placed them on his dressing table. He murmered, "Hail Mary—full of shit. . . ."

The Rolls-Royce was parked outside the entrance to the church. Mae sat in the backseat between Villon and Mallory. Seymour Steel Cheeks was wondering what had compelled this sudden urge of Mae's to go to church. And it was Friday, not Sunday. On Sunday they went to church on the reservation. The kids never wanted to go, but if they remonstrated they were rewarded with the whack of a wet towel.

"It ain't much of a church, is it?" drawled Mae. "That's why I'm so generous with my donations. It's limited seatin' in there, which don't do much for the box office. Listen, boys, I got to tell you somethin' that's on my mind. I hope I don't sound like no hypocrite, which I ain't. I wish it was anybody but Father Wally. I have a soft spot in my heart for him. I think I always will. Him and the rabbi have affected me, each in his own way. It sometimes makes me wish I was more religious."

Villon said, "Mae, I think in your own way, you are."

She patted his cheek. "Give me a few minutes to settle into the confessional and then come tiptoein' in. And please, gentlemen, try not to hurt him." She held out her hand to Villon. He placed his bat's head ring on her palm. She put it in her handbag where it was easily accessible. "Seymour! I'm ready to enter the church."

He was out of the car and on the sidewalk, opening the door for Mae. On the sidewalk, she looked at the handsome Indian who was nursing a brutal hangover. "Seymour, I've seen you lookin' better. You should lay off the firewater." She patted his cheek. "I think it's time to maybe give you a little annuity."

Annuity! At last! Annuity! He watched her sauntering up the walk to the church entrance. Bells should be ringing, thought Seymour, bells, lots of bells. Saint Mae is giving me an annuity!

Once inside the church, Mae's eyes swept the interior. Shabby little house of worship. It could use a couple of coats of paint. Pieces had been carved out of the backs and armrests of some pews. Several of the stained-glass windows had cracks in them. I suppose the condition of this place is enough to drive anyone to murder, thought Mae. She strolled down the aisle to the confessional. Once seated, she pressed the buzzer with her index finger, which bore the weight of an enormous diamond. There were diamond rings on eight fingers. They gave her comfort, the kind of comfort she could never expect from a priest. She heard Father Riggs take his place on the opposite side of the grille. She wet her lips. She opened her hand and stared at the ring. Finally, after taking a deep breath, she spoke.

"Forgive me, Father, for I have sinned."

"Yes, my child." His voice was soft and strained.

"This has been weighin' heavily on me for a long time and after some tragic events last night, I knew it was time to get it off my chest. Well, you see, here's the scenario that I'm dictatin' to you. I'm as much responsible for these here impersonator killin's as the murderer is. If I hadn't convinced his kid brother he belonged in the drag queen business, all them unfortunates would be alive today and struttin' their stuff like they was me, which unfortunately they ain't and never will be." She reached into her purse and found a perfumed handkerchief, which she held to her nose. "What you're smellin' is my special perfume, *Noche de Diablo*. The Night of the Devil. The Devil's been havin' an awful lot of night's these past couple of months. Too damn—sorry—many of them."

Villon and Mallory had entered quietly, and just as quietly walked down the carpeted aisle where they positioned themselves a few feet from Mae's side of the confessional. They could hear her clearly.

"But, Father, that don't excuse the murderer for the awful things he's done. Five victims. Now, that's a disgrace. And, Father, I don't want to drag this on—no pun intended—much longer, because you know I know you're the killer and I'm gonna tell you how come I know. You slipped up twice last night at the Tailspin. When it turned out Connery might not be a Catholic, you said 'Perhaps the person in the garden.' Nobody knew then that Billie Doux was dead in the garden exceptin' me and the cops. And then when you were told Billie was a Catholic for sure, you headed straight for the garden before I could tell Simon LeGrand to direct you there. So you already knew the way to the garden because you'd been there killin' Billie Doux. And in my handbag I've got the twin of that bat's head ring your kid brother bought at the Witches' Brew to give you as a gift.

"Father, you shouldn't have been ashamed of Neon. He was a great talent. And if you really wanted him out of the racket, you should have revealed your true identity to me and you would have won me over to your side. But you were too heated up with anger to reveal your true identity. If you had, that poor kid brother of yours would be alive today. You—"

The screech that filled the church was the cry of a demented banshee. Villon and Mallory watched with amazement as Father Riggs came out of the confessional, face twisted with hatred, on his index finger, the bat's head ring with its deadly fangs exposed. In his left hand, the priest held a knife.

She said in her soft drawl, "Father, I don't like the look of that knife."

He moved toward her with menace. She didn't flinch. She saw Villon and Mallory coming up behind him. They wrestled him to the floor. Seymour Steel Cheeks, curious to see what was going on, came into the church. "Seymour!" Mae shouted. "Give the boys a hand." She stepped out of the confessional and watched Villon pin the priest's hands behind his back and handcuff them. Then the priest was helped to his feet, sobbing,

195

fighting for breath, and staring at Mae with the kind of hatred she hoped never to see again. "Seymour, go find a phone and call the precinct."

"That's not necessary," said Villon. "There's a couple of squad cars parked around the corner."

"You think of everythin', don't you."

"Mae, if I was to tell you some of the things I think about, it might bring a blush to your cheeks."

"Oh, yeah? Why don'tcha try me?"

Father Riggs said to Mae with an ugly snarl, "I should have killed you *first!*" and was hurried away.

"I should have killed you first."

Mae stared at the man as he was guided out. *I should have killed you first.* Never before had she heard or experienced such hatred. She was stunned. After all those checks she gave him!

Mae sat in a pew and commanded, "Seymour! Gimme them smellin' salts!" For the first time in a long time, she was fighting back tears.